THE ANGEL OF PARAGON

USA TODAY BESTSELLING AUTHOR

GENEVIEVE JACK

ABOUT THIS BOOK

An angel called. A devil answered.

Princess Charlotte is the sole heir to the kingdom of Paragon. But twenty-five years after she helped vanquish Empress Eleanor, her parents still treat her like a child—and it doesn't help that her sunny angel disposition makes her easy to overlook. When the king and queen leave Paragon for an extended period, Charlie decides to prove her leadership skills by throwing a party themed around a popular Earth holiday.

Environmental scientist Liam Morris doesn't do relationships *or* celebrations. In his experience, relationships are nothing but distractions, most of them doomed to fail. Pair that with a celebration... No, thank you. He'd rather spend his days on an iceberg in the Arctic than around a table with his family.

Things get complicated when Charlie snatches Liam from Earth and brings him to Paragon, hoping he'll help her iron out the details of her event. Will grumpy, bearded Liam be the answer to her prayers... or more trouble than she can handle?

"Happy birthday, Aunt Avery!" Charlie proudly handed over the gift she'd made her aunt and added a kiss to her cheek for good measure. She'd spent hours designing the set of sapphire earrings—finding the perfect stones, mounting them in gold wire, then charming them with a spell she'd performed herself so that they'd always glow from within. She thought they were a suitable gift for a Highland lady. Charlie had taken care to choose a stone that complemented her aunt's and Xavier's clan colors.

Avery gasped when she opened the box. "Oh, Charlie, they're exquisite!"

Her cheeks warmed. She'd never been good at accepting compliments, but there was nothing better in her estimation than bringing a smile to someone's face. "Thank you. I made them dangle so that your powers wouldn't neutralize the magic that makes them glow."

Avery's innate ability as a witch was to nullify magic, although that particular power wasn't nearly as impressive as her skill with her sword, Fairy Killer. With it in her hand, no dragon, including her mate Xavier, would ever challenge her. Aunt Avery was a total badass.

But she'd also slowed down in recent years. Charlie had noticed that she trained less and slept more when she came to visit these days. With the silver that had appeared in her aunt's hair and the fine lines and wrinkles that edged her eyes and mouth, Charlie couldn't help but notice that Avery was the only person in her life who was aging. Perhaps that's why her mother, Raven, and her father, Gabriel, had invited Xavier and Avery to this special birthday dinner at the Obsidian Palace. Birthdays mattered to Aunt Avery because, as a mortal, she'd only get so many of them.

And Aunt Avery was fifty years old today.

A lump formed in Charlie's throat thinking about it. She'd read humans could live to be a hundred or more, but she didn't like to think that her aunt had an expiration date. And what would happen to Xavier after she was gone? Dragons mated for life—their life, not the lives of their mate. He would never love again after Avery. Just the thought sent a twinge of grief through her heart.

Charlie forced herself to smile brighter. The last thing her aunt needed was to be reminded of their dark future on her special day. She disguised the lump in her throat by focusing her attention on the birthday cake that remained on her plate—a scrumptious earthly tradition she no longer had an appetite for.

Age was a funny thing. Technically, Charlie was twenty-five human years old if she counted using her aunt's age as a guide, but she'd been fully grown for over a decade. Her accelerated maturity was due to celestial magic, the product of being the daughter of a witch and a dragon. In Earth terms, her kind were often called angels, but in the ancient Greek texts in the palace library, she was called a guardian. Neither term suited her. Charlie preferred not to label herself as anything but Charlie, princess of Paragon. Unlike Avery, she was immortal. She'd stopped aging years ago, when she'd surpassed her mother in height and was just shy of being as tall as her father.

"I have one more gift for you, Avery." Raven glanced at Gabriel conspiratorially. Charlie's mother and father were always doing that, speaking to each other without saying anything. What she wouldn't give to be able to read their minds some days.

Dressed in the kilt and linen shirt that was common in his realm and looking serious, Uncle Xavier placed a hand on Avery's shoulder, as if he knew what was coming and was as anxious as he was excited about it. Charlie wondered what it might be.

Her mother and Uncle Nathaniel had argued about something recently and Avery's name had come up, but Charlie hadn't caught the crux of their disagreement.

"Don't keep me in suspense." Avery placed her hand atop Xavier's, glancing between him and Mom as if she was having an equally difficult time guessing what this might be about.

Mom rubbed her palms together in slow circles and rose from her chair to pace the dining room. Charlie tracked her movements. Odd. That's how her mom acted when she was nervous about something. "We think we've found a way for you to take Xavier's tooth."

Avery's face crumpled into a mixture of disappointment and annoyance. "Xavier and I have already tried everything, Raven," she grumbled. "It's time for all of us to accept that I won't be here forever. It's folly to keep trying. It just sets everyone up for disappointment."

Charlie's mother was a powerful witch. If she thought there was a way, there probably was, but Charlie empathized with her aunt's predicament too. Raising everyone's hopes only to fail again and again must be devastating. Mom took a deep breath and let it out through her nose. "I know it seems like we've tried everything, but I've been working with the witches of Darnuith, aided by Queen Penelope. I believe we've found a way. And the best part is, we know it will work because it already has."

Charlie's heart beat faster at the hope her mother offered, but her aunt Avery seemed far less enthusiastic about the possibility. "Darnuith? You told Queen Penelope about my mortality?"

"Penelope is going to perform the spell to unbind the three of us again—you, Clarissa, and me—as Aborella once did. Once your power is gone, Xavier will feed you his tooth. We'll wait for the dragon bond to take hold, then rebind ourselves and return our magic."

A dragon's tooth could make another being immortal for as long as the dragon lived. Rowan's mate, Nick; Nathaniel's mate, Clarissa; Sylas's mate, Dianthe; and Colin's mate, Leena, had all become immortal in this way. But Avery's innate power meant the magic of Xavier's tooth was neutralized by her own before it could take root. Taking away her power long enough for the two to make the immortal bond was a brilliant idea.

Only, judging by the way Avery shifted in her seat, squaring her shoulders as if readying herself for battle, it was clear she didn't share Charlie's fondness for the idea. "Absolutely not!" Avery snapped. "The three of us will be defenseless."

"Only temporarily." Mom started pacing again. Beside her, Dad had gone unnervingly still, a behavior Charlie recognized was the calm before the storm. He was becoming agitated, and she suspected he wouldn't be quiet for long.

"You'll be at the mercy of Darnuith," Avery gritted out. "All Penelope would need to do is kill us all when we're vulnerable and she could take Paragon."

A deep roar cut through her father's throat. *There he goes.* Charlie had to stop herself from leaning away from him in her seat. He'd never been anything but kind to her, but that growl was a threat she could feel in her bones.

"Last I checked, I am still king of Paragon, and I have no intention of handing the kingdom over so easily. No one will hurt Raven or a single hair on the heads of the three of you because I, along with Xavier and Nathaniel, will be there to make sure they don't. Three mate-bonded dragons are something no intelligent ruler would intentionally antagonize."

Raven placed a calming hand on Gabriel's arm and added, "Penelope has proven herself a trustworthy ally. She's one of my best friends, and as queen she knows that this will put us in her kingdom's debt. Believe me, Avery, I wouldn't have pursued this if I thought it wasn't safe. There is risk, and it won't be easy, but I believe it will work. She'll take apart the bond, we'll lose our powers, Xavier will feed you his tooth, and then the witches will bond us again, as was done before. Nathaniel will be there himself to oversee all of it."

Xavier gripped his mate's shoulders and shook

gently. "Ye've got ta try, *mo chridhe*. It'll kill ma ta lose ya, ye ken? I won' 'ave it. Nah without a fight."

The lump was back in Charlie's throat as a tear cut a trail down Avery's cheek. It was all there in those stormy eyes. She could dismiss her sister, but she'd try anything for her mate.

"Fine. I'll do it." Her aunt took a deep breath, her inner warrior seeming to wake up to the idea. "But for the record, I don't think anyone should get their hopes up." She directed that at Raven and Xavier with a steely glance at one, then the other. "It's possible that as soon as I have my powers returned, the effects of the tooth will be neutralized and we'll be back where we started. All of us need to prepare ourselves for a disappointing outcome."

Behind her, Xavier's mouth hooked into a grin. "Ach, I prefer ta hope fur the best."

"It's settled then," Gabriel said. "I'll ask Marius to man the kingdom in our absence."

Up to that point, Charlie had been content observing from the sidelines and praying Aunt Avery would attempt her mother's plan, but her father's words brought her back into the moment. She smiled up at her father and cleared her throat. "No need to ask Marius," she said brightly. "*I* will head the kingdom in your absence."

Her mother paused, looking flustered. "Oh, Charlie, Marius has a wealth of experience from his work as ambassador. I'm sure he won't mind."

She shook her head. "I don't mind. Marius is busy with his own duties as well as his family. I am princess, and I have no other responsibilities. I'm happy to do it."

"Well, that's so sweet of you, Charlie, really, but, uh—" Raven glanced at Gabriel as if pleading for him to back her up.

A dull ache started in Charlie's chest as she slowly came to suspect that her mother either didn't think she was capable of leading the kingdom in her absence or didn't trust her with the responsibility. "I am a fully grown adult. Older, in fact, than you were when you had me—"

"But you've never done something like this before," Raven argued breathlessly. "And we'll be gone two to three weeks. Maybe longer."

"We will?" Avery flashed her sister a confused look.

"We need to give the tooth time to become part of you," Raven explained. "Penelope says that if the magic is given time to root in all your cells that when your abilities return, they won't recognize it as something foreign. Only we don't know exactly how long that will take."

Avery closed her eyes for a beat as if she found the idea overwhelming.

Charlie made use of the silence that followed to continue to plead her case. In a kind but confident tone, she said, "I understand why you'd be worried, but I've participated in every aspect of running this kingdom from your side for no less than five years. I know the ins and outs as well as anyone, and aside from one meeting of the Elder Council, which I can lead in my sleep, there is nothing but managing the house on the royal schedule at the moment. Besides, it's not as if Marius won't be here if I have questions. And if by some twist of fate he's unavailable, Alexander and Maiara are still in residence, and Colin and Leena are too."

"She has a point," Gabriel murmured, eliciting a pained look from her mother.

Aunt Avery and Xavier became suspiciously quiet as they no doubt attempted to avoid getting caught up in the family tiff. Charlie hadn't meant to make anyone uncomfortable—it just seemed obvious to her that this was her job and one she could easily do.

Her mother coupled her hands in front of her hips. "Listen… Charlie… You're right. You are ready, but why don't we let Marius take this one, and then when your father and I return, we can gradually transition more responsibilities to you and create some opportunities for you to practice your leadership skills during shorter absences and under more controlled circumstances."

A deep well of disappointment opened in Charlie's chest. "You don't think I can do it."

"That's not what your mother is suggesting," her father said. "We want to be fair to you. I've managed people for most of my existence, and I would never spring a responsibility of this magnitude on someone of your age and experience with this short notice."

Charlie could hear the note of finality in her father's voice and frowned at the floor, knowing that the decision had already been made. As disappointing as it was to her, the last thing Charlie wanted was to be a burden on her parents during this already difficult time. If they were worried about the kingdom, they wouldn't be free to concentrate on the spell that could save her aunt. She'd only wanted to help, not to cause them more worry.

"All right," she said softly.

Her mother gave her shoulder an empathetic pat. "I'll tell Marius to allow you to lead Elder Council and to lean on you as much as he needs to."

Charlie's smile was shaky as she replied, "Okay. I understand."

"Then it's settled." Her mother turned back to her sister. "Avery, Xavier, let's plan to leave first thing in the morning."

Avery clutched Xavier's hand, her lashes fluttering. "Three weeks means we'll miss Christmas in the *builgean.*"

Xavier shook his head. "If this works, it'll be the greatest gift ya could bestow 'pon our clan. There'll be other Christmases, *curaidh.*"

Funny, Charlie had participated in a few Christmases with her mother and human grandparents when she was very young, but it had been more than two decades. Once it was deemed dangerous for her to leave Paragon, their family stopped the tradition, even when her grandparents came to visit. She couldn't remember much about the Earth holiday or why it was so important to humans. The way her aunt and uncle were acting, it was a true loss to miss it.

"We should make preparations," her father said before rising to leave the room. Everyone stood to follow, murmuring about what to bring on their royal trip to Darnuith. Charlie was left staring after them, fists clenched. Deep inside, she just knew she was born to lead, and she vowed to someday prove it to them.

TWO

The library of the Obsidian Palace was one of Charlie's favorite places to be. When the palace was renovated after Eleanor was overthrown, her mother and father had doubled its size and one could spend hours perusing three stories of shelves. There was no librarian, but thanks to a clever locator spell, you simply asked the library itself for a book on any topic and she would deliver. (Charlie had always thought of the library as a she, although she knew it wasn't sentient.)

She stood before the perpetual flame at the center of the library and wrote EARTH-DIMENSION CHRISTMAS on a slip of paper. Folding it twice, she tossed it into the flames. A rumble like a minor earthquake shook the floor beneath her feet, and then a book appeared on the table beside the fire.

No title graced the cover or the spine, which

looked to be solid gold and was patterned with a garden scene, but inside, the parchment held passages about Earth history and folklore. Charlie carried it to one of the long wooden tables at the center of the library and sat down to flip through the pages for an entry on Christmas. They'd celebrated Avery's birthday with an Earth cake. Maybe there was something Charlie could do to lessen the sting of missing this other Earth holiday.

"Christmas... Christmas..."

"There you are." Marius entered the library behind her, his eyes drooping like he hadn't slept in days. The baby on his shoulder had no such issue. She was sound asleep, her tiny features and round cheeks perfectly peaceful. Olivia had hatched only a few moon cycles ago, and her sleep schedule seemed to be completely flipped.

"You look exhausted. This little one keeping you on your toes?" Charlie stood and gave her favorite uncle a gentle hug, careful not to disturb Olivia.

Marius grunted. "Thank the Mountain dragons don't need much shuteye. Neither of us are getting much these days. I caught Harlow asleep standing up yesterday. Right in front of the sink with the water running, out cold."

Charlie grimaced. "I heard you pacing the halls with her outside my room last night. Or I should say I heard *her*. An incredible set of lungs on this little beasty."

"Sorry to wake you. I was trying to take her far enough away from our chambers she wouldn't wake Harlow and the other whelps. But these obsidian halls carry sound like nobody's business."

"No worries." Charlie shot him a commiserative smile. "If you ever want to leave her with me for a night so you two can catch up on some sleep, I'd be happy to take her."

"Mountain, that is generous of you. Harlow told me to bring her to try to wake her up so she'd sleep tonight, but you can see how that's going. The Mountain herself could erupt and this one would snooze through it during the day."

With a supportive pat to his shoulder, she grinned. "You are doing an excellent job, Marius... An excellent job convincing me never to have children."

They both laughed, although inside her chest, a deep sadness bubbled under the surface. Children were something she doubted she'd ever have to worry about. She didn't have much of a romantic life to speak of. Although she was a princess and had been told she was beautiful by dragon standards, she was not a dragon, and her would-be suitors in the kingdom had balked at her feathery white wings and inability to shift. Aside from a few kisses at royal gatherings, she'd had only one true lover, a vampire from Nochtbend who'd lost interest once they'd had sex and he'd tasted her blood. She'd agreed to the bite, not knowing that her blood, seeped in her magic, carried an electric charge that burned his mouth. He'd stopped courting her after that.

Charlie gave herself a mental shake and glanced at her uncle. "Um, it sounded like you were looking for me?"

Marius's eyes had gone blank for a moment. He started, running a hand down his face. "Yes. I spoke with Raven before the group left for Darnuith this morning, and she told me to let you lead Elder Council next week. As far as I'm concerned, I'm happy for you to help with whatever you'd like to help with. I'm surprised your mom and dad didn't leave the palace in your hands, honestly. You're more than capable."

"Thanks, Uncle Marius. I appreciate that. You can count on me to help in any way you need." Her gaze flicked toward her toes. "To be honest, I was disappointed they wouldn't leave me in charge, but the spell they're doing with Avery is very stressful for them all. I'm sure it's more about them than about what they think of me."

He squeezed her shoulder supportively. "It's very mature of you to put their feelings ahead of your own. But I want you to know that as their delegate, I need your help. I'll have a schedule sent over. Maybe you can manage the morning staff and I'll do the evening shift, when I'm up anyway."

"Done," she said confidently. It wasn't like the palace needed much managing. The staff had it running like clockwork.

Marius gave her a nod as if they'd reached some sort of formal agreement. She'd always been exceptionally close to Marius since the time he'd rescued her from the underworld when she was just discovering her powers. She wondered if he actually needed help or if this was his way of soothing the burn of her parent's decision. If it was, she loved him even more for it.

"What are you doing in here anyway?" he asked.

She placed a hand on the book and quirked a smile. "You're going to think it's dumb."

"I highly doubt that. You're a brilliant girl, Charlie. Nothing you're interested in is dumb."

As always, her cheeks warmed at the compliment, but her wings might have plumped a little too. "I thought it would be nice to put on a Christmas for Avery and Xavier."

"A *Christmas*? Oh, isn't that some sort of Earth celebration?"

She nodded. "I heard Avery tell Xavier that they'd miss the holiday while they were in Darnuith performing the spell. She seemed really disappointed. Technically I could probably time walk them back a few weeks so that they could experience it with their clan, but I thought it would be a fun surprise if I threw a Christmas here instead. We can celebrate what hopefully will be her newly won immortality in a way she's comfortable. I'm sure Mom and Clarissa would appreciate it too, considering they grew up on Earth."

Marius's gaze warmed tenderly. "Incredibly thoughtful. And smart about avoiding the time walking. It's dangerous."

She shrugged. "Not as dangerous as it used to be."

He cleared his throat and changed the subject. "How does one throw a Christmas? I admit I know nothing about Earth celebrations. Harlow and I had an Earth wedding, but Raven planned the entire thing. All I can guess is that there's probably cake. Humans have a cake for everything."

"I remember your wedding cake!" She giggled. "And Mom made Avery a smaller version to celebrate her fifty-year birth anniversary. It was good too."

He nodded. "So maybe a cake for their return."

"But what makes it a Christmas cake?"

He shrugged.

"That's why I'm here. I'm doing research. The library sent me this book, so hopefully there's something here I can use."

A yawn stretched Marius's mouth. "You should talk to Alexander. He lived there for centuries. Plus he's an artist, so he could draw you exactly what it should look like."

"Oh, good point." She rubbed her chin. Her uncle Tobias and aunt Rowan and their mates would have had plenty of experience with Earth Christmas too, but they were busy with their own lives. Truth was, she didn't want to ask for help, not even from Alexander. It was too hard to explain to Marius that the entire point of throwing this party was to prove to her parents that she could handle organizing something complex and original on her own. If one of her relatives was involved, it would be too easy for her mom and dad to assume they'd done most of the work for her. She had to do this herself.

"Did someone say my name?" Alexander appeared in the door of the library, dressed in torn Earth jeans, a white T-shirt, and the paint-splattered leather jacket he was rarely seen without—Earth garb the artist refused to give up. He nodded at Marius. "Harlow sent me to find you. Seems Archie's got his head stuck in the chair again, and she needs your help getting him out."

Archie was Harlow's second youngest and was going through a phase where he was into everything. Marius closed his eyes and gave his head one hard shake. "That boy is going to drive me back to the fighting pits. We didn't have these problems with Anissa."

"Anissa was an only child," Charlie added. Anissa was Marius's firstborn and a single egg. She was already grown and away at university. Archie was from Harlow's second pregnancy, one of three children and the only boy. Annabelle and Aria were absolute angels, but Archie never missed a chance at trouble. Olivia was the result of Harlow's third pregnancy, a rarity for dragons, and aside from never sleeping at night, seemed just as sweet as her sisters.

"How does one get their head stuck in a chair?" Alexander asked.

Charlie laughed, picturing the pudge-faced Archie in his predicament.

Marius's lips slanted in an adorably frustrated way before he answered. "Take a chair with widely spaced spindles and add a boy with an oddly narrow skull who can't stay out of trouble and somehow it happens. This is the third time he's done it. You'd think he'd learn by now. I'm starting to believe he might like it, to be honest." He headed for the door at a fast clip.

She called her goodbyes after him and Olivia, who drooled on his shoulder, still in dreamland.

"Has his hands full." Alexander chuckled. "Times like these, I remind myself why it's probably a blessing Maiara and I can't have children. I do not envy him, you know?"

She giggled. "I enjoy children, but I also like to sleep. Maybe in a hundred years if I ever meet the right male."

Alexander pumped a fist in solidarity. "So what did you want to ask me about? I heard you mention my name."

She hesitated for a moment. It wouldn't hurt to ask—she simply wouldn't accept his help if he offered. "Do you know anything about Christmas?"

"The Earth-dimension holiday?"

"Exactly the one. I want to throw one for Avery and Xavier when they return."

Alexander thought about that for a moment. "Can't say that I do. I never celebrated the holiday myself when I lived there. My mate is from a different culture, one that did not know Christmas, and I never had a reason to participate."

"Oh. Never mind then. I'll think of something."

He gave her a shallow bow, then left the room.

"Looks like you are my only hope," she said to the book. She grabbed a pad of paper and a quill from the library desk, then started sifting through the pages. "Christmas... Christmas..."

She found the entry under religious holidays near the back of the book. *Christmas is both a religious and secular holiday celebrated by humans. Some believe it is the birthday of the son of one of their gods. Others celebrate a celestial being who lives at the North Pole of their planet, where it is always winter. This being is called Saint Nicholas or Santa Claus and is often depicted wearing a red suit and having a beard. If children are good all year, he magically knows and rewards them with a toy that he leaves in their home on Christmas eve night.*

Charlie furrowed her brow. "He breaks into people's homes in the middle of the night to leave gifts? Weird." She made a list on the notepad. *Demigod. North Pole. Red suit. Beard.* She underlined the name *Santa Claus* three times. It wasn't much to go on. Why wasn't there anything about cake? She really wanted this to be good. She wanted her parents and her aunts to see what she had done and know that she was a capable adult and worthy leader. A true princess of Paragon.

She flipped through the gold book again but could find no other information on the subject. Tapping her thumb on the notebook, she wondered where she should look next. Leena might be able to find information for her in the scrolls of Rogos or gaze into a pool of the goddess's tears to scry it for her. But that would mean bothering the scribe, who was always incredibly busy. Plus she very much wanted to accomplish this on her own.

Studying her notes yet again, a wave of excitement washed through her as an idea brightened the corners of her mind. The answer was right in front of her. Santa Claus was a celestial being who lived at the North Pole! Charlie was also a celestial being, one who could travel between dimensions and was impervious to extreme heat or cold.

She didn't need help or another reference manual. All she needed was Santa Claus.

THREE

The beam from Dr. Liam Morris's headlamp lit a circle of ice below him as he guided the ice auger into position. Inside the space-suit-style gear he was wearing, he didn't feel the cold, but the wind was another story. He leaned into an especially strong gust, gripping the auger, which was thankfully mounted to his Arctic rover, for support. A light snow had started, but the sky was threatening a full storm. He needed to hurry. Even with his specialized equipment, he'd rather not face the full brutality of this unforgiving environment. The North Pole was encased in total darkness this time of year, and he was one of only a handful of scientists on the planet willing and able to brave it for the sake of science.

This excursion was absolutely necessary for his research. Satellite surveillance could tell a lot about the shifting ice in the Arctic, how thick and wide it was at various points during the year, but the composition of that ice when it was at its thickest was what interested Liam. Knowing what microbial and chemical components composed the layers and how that mix was different from the year before would go a long way in understanding how the earth was changing, how concentrated the pollution in the ocean was at this remote location, and the potential dangers to come.

He locked the specially designed auger into place, a more difficult job than it seemed thanks to his thick gloves, and entered the code to start the extraction. His suit had a system to warm the air inside his helmet, which made his breathing sound like Darth Vader's, and he concentrated on the sound to calm himself as he worked. Then there was nothing to do but wait for the extraction program to run its course.

"Liam, you still with me, buddy?" The intercom in his helmet transmitted the voice of his partner, Noah.

"Still here. Charge on the rover is good. All vitals good. Sample extraction is at ten minutes, twenty seconds and counting."

"Excellent." Static buzzed in his ear. "So what did your fiancée think of you coming on this expedition over the holidays?"

Just like Noah to get personal when he had nothing to do but wait and maintain communication. "My *ex*-fiancée was more than happy to hear I was going to the ends of the earth, although I think she'd be happier if I jumped off it."

"Ouch."

"Honestly, I don't give a shit what she thinks. Breaking it off was a relief. Marriage is a sham, Noah. The only people who want to be married are those who would benefit from the social contract. She wanted the Morris name, both for the publicity and for the money she thought I was worth. Boy, if you could have seen her face when I told her the real story. She couldn't throw the ring at me fast enough."

"Wait, wasn't she an underwear model or something?"

"Yeah, lingerie. She was also a body double for Marie Swiftfleet in that movie *Exodus*." Liam fully admitted he was a sucker for feminine beauty.

"Seems like you might have benefited from the social contract as well." Noah guffawed into his ear.

"I was attracted to her, sure, and she was a nice enough woman, but Victoria wanted my family name and a bank account to match. She wanted to do the domestic thing. You know, two or three kids, home in the evenings for dinner around the table, and then watch li'l Liam's basketball games."

"Not for you, huh?"

"Just the thought makes me want to take up drinking. I don't think she really ever appreciated what I do. She wanted someone like my brother, not me. Nothing she could give me was worth selling my soul for. Why not just buy a Norman Rockwell calendar and call it a day? Plastic people, plastic families, plastic friendships. You know what plastic does? It pollutes. This kind just pollutes society instead of the oceans."

"I bet you're fun at parties." Noah snorted.

Liam hated parties, but he kept that to himself. No need to give Noah any more ammunition. "Relationships and I don't mix. Maybe someday I'll get a dog, but I'm done with women."

"Oh? That still leaves men, Liam. Robert and I have been together eleven years this Wednesday."

"If only that did it for me," he muttered.

"You're not the domestic type. Understood."

"Nope. I don't know why I ever considered getting married in the first place. I've always been a lone wolf."

"You did not just call yourself a lone wolf!" Now Noah was cackling.

"I don't know how else to put it, my friend. I'm not interested in settling down. I mean sure, I'm a red-blooded male who's as interested in sex as the next guy, but spending a lifetime with just one woman... Where's the discovery in that? Besides, a regular nine-to-five with a couple brats swinging from my arms is never going to cut it for me."

"So with Victoria out of the picture, will you be spending the holidays with your family on the estate this year?"

The Morris family estate was no doubt decked out

in holiday splendor by now, the staff ready to host the entire clan... but him. An unwelcome ache started in his chest. Why did he even care anymore? The last time he'd seen his mother in person—it had to have been almost a year ago now—she'd been especially cruel, telling him he'd never amount to anything spending his days trying to save the planet. He hadn't been close to his parents in over a decade, not since he found out about "the secret." Hadn't even attended his father's funeral in August.

It's why he'd jumped at the chance to perform this field research now. Although they'd be back in time for Christmas, it was close enough to be a viable excuse for nonattendance. Deep down, he didn't want to deal with his mother or his family anymore. He'd rather be on a block of ice in the darkest part of the world than sitting around a gilded table among a sea of fake smiles and giant egos.

Only, something bothered him about this year. "You know, I'd prefer to beg off, but weirdly enough, my mother called me just before we left Chicago. She says there's something of dire importance she needs to share with Spencer, Kara, and me."

"So are you going to go?" Noah asked.

Liam frowned. "Maybe. Mom has never been the overly sentimental type. If she uses the words *dire importance*, she means them. I'm just not convinced whatever it is will be important enough to me to bother attending."

"Aww, come on, Liam. She's your mom and it's Christmas."

"Yeah." He blinked, looking up at the stars. The auger beeped, and he cast his unwanted feelings aside to tend to the gathered sample, swinging it into the receptacle on the rover. Nothing made him happier than concentrating on work, compartmentalizing the family and relationship stuff. None of that mattered in the grand scheme of things, did it? What he was doing here was far more important.

Bright light glared through the side of his helmet, driving out his deep thoughts and engulfing his rover in a warm ecru glow. Confused, he turned to find the source and blinked rapidly against the glare. Had another university sent an expedition? Or was this some billionaire seeking an adrenaline high?

Liam's eyes finally adjusted, and he saw clearly where the light was coming from. He stopped breathing. The alarm went off in his suit as his heart sprinted into the tachycardic zone.

"Liam, what's going on? Your heart rate is off the charts!" Noah's panicked voice barked in his ear.

Liam wanted to answer, but he couldn't get his mouth to work properly. He tried again. "Wo-wo—" He swallowed hard and forced his tongue to obey him. "A woman. There's a... a woman out here."

"Who? Is there a logo on her suit? Not that Russian scientist again."

"No suit. She's barefoot... in a fucking dress," he

forced out. He blinked rapidly, trying to make sense of what he was seeing.

"If there was a woman out there in nothing but a dress right now, she'd be frozen solid," Noah said. "Check your oxygen. Your stats look fine from here, but something must be going on."

What was going on was the most beautiful woman he'd ever seen was walking toward him, barefoot in a white dress that hugged her figure, her loose blond waves blowing back from her face in the mounting storm. The only thing stranger than the fact she didn't look cold were the two massive, feathery wings rising over her shoulders and the glow she was putting off, which set off a blaring rendition of Aerosmith's "Angel" in his brain.

She was an angel—he was sure of it—but he couldn't say the word. To say it out loud to Noah would mean he believed it, and he hadn't believed in angels since he was a child. He glanced down at his monitor to check his vitals. Oxygen fine. Breathing and pulse fast but steady. Temperature normal. He blinked twice before turning his gaze toward her again. And finding her standing right in front of him.

She placed her hands on either side of his helmet. Her mouth moved, but he couldn't make out what she was saying through the visor. He tapped against the side of the helmet over his ear, trying to make her understand. Her hands gripped his upper arms and shook. Looking directly through his visor with piercing blue eyes, she said, *I need your help*! At least he thought that's what she said based on reading her lips.

He nodded immediately. Of course he would help this lovely creature who should not exist and was probably a figment of his oxygen-deprived imagination. Or maybe, he thought chillingly, he was already dead, and this angel was here to take him to the beyond. Shit luck if that was the case. He didn't think he'd be going to the good place considering he hadn't set foot in a church in years.

He drew a deep breath and wiggled his fingers. He didn't *feel* dead. In fact, his heart was beating so hard it pounded in his ears like a bass drum.

The woman distracted him again with a smile that lit up the night. He'd made her happy, although he wasn't sure how. For some reason that meant the world to him. Pivoting, she slashed a hand through the night, drawing a symbol with the strange light that surrounded her. His breath hitched as the darkness seemed to curl away like the edges of burnt parchment. She hooked her arm into his and tugged him forward. One giant step to catch his balance... and he was standing inside a symbol on the floor of an entirely black room. The North Pole was gone, and he was... He was...

Suddenly unable to breathe and feeling like he was going to be sick, he frantically grasped at the seal to his helmet, managing to pry it off his head just in time.

He bent over at the waist, emptying the contents of his stomach on the shiny black floor.

"...entirely normal," he heard a woman say from behind him, but when he tried to turn to look at her, the room tilted and the floor rose up and bit him in the head.

"Ow," he said under his breath.

"Oh!" he heard the woman yell as she rushed to his side. Her stunningly beautiful face was the last thing he saw before the darkness closed in around him.

FOUR

"*F*uck, *fuck, fuck!*" Charlie checked to make sure the demigod was still breathing before cleaning the sick off the floor of her ritual room. She hadn't expected him to react to dimension hopping as he had. It was normal to feel woozy after crossing time and space, but she'd assumed the magical being would have a stronger constitution. But when he'd removed his head covering, she'd realized that perhaps the differences between their worlds were more than she'd accounted for.

"Eww." She ditched the rags into her cauldron, and with a snap of her fingers and a spoken incantation, they burst into flames. Mercifully, the man hadn't gotten any on himself, but his skin was covered in a sheen of sweat. Then again, maybe that wasn't from the hop. After inspecting the padded red suit he was in, she decided it must be designed for the frigid weather where he was from. She had to get him out of it so he could cool off and she could make sure he was okay.

Thank goodness supernatural strength was one of her gifts because he was enormous. With some effort, she rolled him onto his side and released the strange clasps holding the thick material together. Once it was open, she slid him out of the awkward outfit and took her first look at the being the humans called Santa Claus.

He wasn't what she'd been expecting.

Saint Nick was built like a dragon, although perhaps slightly smaller than her uncles. Nonetheless, he was tall and broad, as big as a Darnuthian mountain bear with arms as thickly corded as her uncle Colin's, which was saying something considering he was the Master of the Guard. She could see his muscles clearly thanks to the strange, stretchy red fabric shirt and tights he wore. Other parts of his anatomy were equally visible and just as well developed. The sight made her throat feel thick, and she cleared it before wrestling her gaze back up to his face.

The magic man wasn't just as big as a bear, he also looked like a bear with a thick, dark wild beard that matched scraggly, overgrown hair. She wrinkled her nose. Such an odd, untamed appearance.

Why was he still unconscious? His powers must truly be limited to gifts and teleportation for the dimension walk to affect him like this. Perhaps he hadn't realized his agreement to help her came with interdimensional travel. *Stupid, Charlie! You didn't explain it clearly enough to him. Could he even hear you inside that suit?*

What if he woke up angry at her? Chewing her lip, she twisted a strand of her hair around her finger, pulling it tight until the tip turned white. This was, perhaps, not the smartest thing she'd ever done. When she'd asked him for help, he'd nodded eagerly, but it was possible he hadn't understood what she had in mind.

With a sigh, she brushed the thought aside. Worrying about it wouldn't solve anything, and he wouldn't thank her for leaving him on the floor. Bending her knees, she scooped him into her arms and carried him into her bedroom, arranging him in the bed and covering him with a sheet. At least now he'd be comfortable when he woke, and then they could discuss her plan—celestial being to celestial being.

A few seconds later, he shifted his head on the pillow and she breathed a sigh of relief. If he'd stayed under much longer, she'd have no choice but to fetch the healer, and the last thing she wanted to do was explain this to Maiara. She leaned over him, studying his gruff, oversized exterior and hoping that when he did open his eyes, he'd forgive her for the rough journey. His lids fluttered open, and the immediate scowl on his face had her taking a step back.

"Who the fuck are you, and what have you done

to me?"

LIAM TOOK A DEEP BREATH, HIS LIDS FEELING HEAVY AS HE awaited an answer. When he'd first woken up, the warm air and cool sheets told him he must be in the medical bay of the research station. He was convinced the entire thing was a nightmare. Noah was going to give him so much shit for whatever mistake he'd made that had led to the hallucinations.

But when he'd forced his eyes open, expecting to see fluorescent lights and gray medical cabinets, he'd found himself again staring into the face of an angel. The same winged woman he'd seen walking barefoot across the ice stood over him now, looking deeply concerned. He'd asked who she was, his heart racing as he started fully awake, then slid into the headboard, sitting up to put space between them.

She squinted at him as if *he* was the strangest thing in this room, as if the wings and the abrupt change in scenery required no explanation. How long had he been out? She must have hit him over the head and airlifted him out of there. He glanced at the window. It was possible he was in Norway.

"What kind of god are *you*?" she asked.

"Wh-what?" He'd never been asked such an insane question. "If you're joking, this isn't funny. You interrupted some seriously important research." This entire situation was beyond comprehension. He scratched his beard and frowned at her feathers. She had them plumped and stretched behind her like a bird guarding its prey. Was that some kind of high-end cosplay?

"This isn't a joke," she said firmly.

"Then what is it? Why have you brought me here?" The last thing he expected from a research trip to the North Pole was to be abducted. "You won't get any money for me, sweetheart. I'm not that important to either my family or my university."

Her wings folded flat behind her—the animatronics were incredible!—and she tucked in her chin quizzically. "I'm not holding you for ransom! Why would you think such a thing?"

"Then why am I here?"

She raised a contemplative eyebrow. "I brought you here because I need your help. I didn't realize you'd have a negative reaction to my powers."

"Powers?" He curled his lip. Not greedy then but crazy. Great. "Why are you dressed in an angel costume?"

She stood straighter. "This is no costume, sir." She turned to the side and wriggled her wings for him.

Slowly his synapses fired and comprehension dawned until there was no doubt they were real. Two feathery miracles growing out of her back.

"Jesus fucking Chri—!" He cut himself off and pressed a hand to his chest, feeling for his heart. "You're a fucking angel? Am I dead? Is this heaven?"

"No!"

"Hell?"

She scoffed. "You're not dead, Nick." She shook her head incredulously. "You're speaking to me and moving around, aren't you? I haven't hurt you. You just passed out."

That was an awfully defensive response from someone who snatched him from his jobsite not too long ago. He scowled. "But... but you *are* an... um, an angel." He finally found the thump, thump of his pulse with his fingers and took a deep, cleansing breath. He was definitely alive, although perhaps losing his mind.

She closed her eyes for a second and gave him a sweet little laugh. "Oh, I see the problem now. You think I'm a heavenly angel as described in your Earth folklore." With a shrug, she spread her hands. "I'm real. A celestial being just like you, Nick. No need to fear, you are perfectly safe and very much alive. I'm sorry I didn't explain more about what I planned to do before we left your realm."

"My realm," he drawled, squinting at her. "Sorry, but I'm still not following. Do you mean my camp? And why do you keep calling me Nick?" A frisson of anger drove out his former fear. Who was she, and why *hadn't* she explained more before she, what, knocked him out and brought him here? And where was here?

His captor's lips twitched into an annoyingly adorable half smile. "Isn't that your name? Saint Nick.

Or..." She looked at a notebook on the desk beside her. "Santa Claus? Do you prefer Santa Claus?"

He stared at her for a few long moments, trying to process what she was saying. She swore this wasn't a joke. Maybe she was insane. Yes, he must operate under the assumption he was dealing with someone not quite right in the head. "My name isn't Nick," he said clearly. "It's Liam. *Doctor* Liam Morris." His voice became even more clipped as he added through his teeth, "And I don't appreciate being abducted from my fieldwork. Who are you, and who do you work for?"

She huffed, flopping her hands down by her sides. "I didn't abduct you! I asked for your help and you nodded—you agreed. And how can you not be Santa Claus? You have a beard." She checked her notebook again. "You were wearing a red suit. And you were at the North Pole!"

He scratched his neck and looked around the room. Aside from the wings, everything around him seemed relatively ordinary. He was lying in a four-poster bed, wearing nothing but his base layer and a purple sheet that matched the comforter. Beyond the foot of the bed was a cozy sitting area bordered by what looked to be a window... No, now that he looked more closely, it was a veranda. Wait, that was impossible. It would take days to get anywhere warm enough for open air, and he was sure he hadn't been out that long. Whomever she was working for couldn't have brought him far unless he'd been out a lot longer than he'd thought. There had to be an explanation. Maybe he was on a ship and the veranda was enclosed in glass. Yes, that must be it. He simply couldn't see the glass from this angle.

"Where are we?" he demanded. He had a theory. Some very wealthy people would love to stop his research from happening. He guessed she worked for them and had injected him with something that rendered him unconscious before she loaded him onto a rover and transported him here. Most likely scenario was that he'd been airlifted to Norway and put on a ship cruising south.

"You are in Paragon," she said. "You're safe here."

"Is that the name of the ship?"

She looked confused for a moment. "You're not on a ship. I brought you here, to my home, because I need your help. We call our world Ouros."

"You..." He had to swallow and lick his lips to go on. "Are you honestly suggesting you brought me to another *world?*" He gave a dark laugh. Now he was sure she was crazy. He couldn't explain the wings, but it was clear she had a screw loose.

"Yes. Ouros. I know this must be disorienting for you as it's clear you're not used to jumping dimensions." She drew her fingers along her temple and through her hair as if she might be any woman in any coffee shop, sharing about her day with him. "Sorry about the side effects—I assumed as a celestial being you'd be more resilient to my magic. But then, it seems

I was wrong about you being a celestial being." She pinched her chin, studying him.

He studied her right back, trying to make sense of any of it. *Think like a crazy person, Liam.* "So you're like an *alien* from another world."

She frowned. "Sort of."

He blinked at her, trying not to laugh. The idea was ridiculous. "Are you going to experiment on me? Needles? Anal probes?"

Her eyes widened. "No!" She tucked in her chin, a disgusted look on her face. "Anal probes? Why?" She squinted, her voice lowering. "Wait, do you want me to?"

"No!" he said firmly, holding up both hands and laughing in earnest now. What a stupid thing for him to say. If she was crazy, the last thing he should have done was give her any ideas. There had to be a rational explanation for all this.

"Good." She gave an endearing little snort. "Thank the Mountain. I was hoping that wasn't some crazy Earth custom."

He stared at her for a beat, trying to get his head around the situation. Fuck, she was cute. Beautiful even. Tall, full breasts, slender, and those eyes! He could lose hours within their depths. Suddenly he was aware of just how long it had been since he'd been with a woman. He shook his head to dismiss the rogue thought. The last thing he should be thinking about was sex, but his abductor was the stuff of fantasies.

His gaze lingered on her rose-colored mouth as his mind sent him a delicious daydream about those full lips wrapped around his cock.

Rubbing his forehead, he broke off that thought as quickly as possible. He should have his head examined for thinking about fucking her right now. What he needed to do was figure a way out of this.

You're a scientist, Liam! Start gathering data! "What's your name?"

"Charlie. Short for Charlotte."

"Charlotte," he murmured.

"Oh, you can call me Charlie. Most people do." A light blush stained her cheeks, and Liam's pulse quickened. Why anyone would call this gorgeous and sophisticated woman a masculine name like Charlie, he had no idea.

"I like Charlotte. You look like a Charlotte." *Get a grip. Was he actually flirting with her?*

"Um, thanks." She flashed him a showstopping smile.

"My name is Liam. Liam Morris. Not Santa Claus. Not Saint Nick. I was at the North Pole because I'm a scientist who studies ice."

"You study frozen water?" She gave a breathy chuckle.

"Yes... Kind of... I'm an environmental scientist who specializes in changing ice formations at the poles."

"Oh."

"My suit is red so that my partner can find me in a snowstorm, and I have a beard because I've been either traveling or working in an Arctic outpost for the past month."

For a second she shifted on her feet, presumably trying to discern if he was telling the truth. Then she released a stream of curses that had no business coming from an angel's mouth. "Do you know where I can find the real Santa Claus?"

He gave a muffled chuckle, then stopped when it became clear that she was serious. "In a storybook," he said firmly. When she looked at him like she didn't understand, he added, "He's not real. He's a story... for children... made up to enhance the holiday season."

Had he really just had to explain to a grown woman that Santa wasn't real?

Charlotte groaned and plopped into the chair behind the desk, holding her head. "This is a disaster."

"The day's not working out that well for me either, sweetheart."

She raised her gaze to his. "I am sorry, Scientist Liam, if I have inconvenienced you by bringing you here. But please don't be alarmed. I can return you to the exact place and point in time when I took you as soon as I'm rested. I promise you I'll make it right."

He was about to lay into her about how her actions had most likely ruined his experiment, time travel being impossible even when someone was rested, and how his partner even now had likely already notified authorities, when a bird the size of a dog flew over her balcony and all the words lodged in his throat. Liam straightened to attention. Was that an eagle or an albatross? It appeared bigger than both. Where in the world was he? The veranda was drenched in sun. There shouldn't be sun this time of year.

On autopilot, he slid his legs over the side of the bed and rose to walk toward the balcony. The floor was polished obsidian, unusual for a ship. He stepped out, into the sun. Where was the glass? Where was the water? This was no ship.

He reached the stone railing bordering the veranda and gaped at the forest beyond it, forcing his brain to grasp that he was not on a vessel at all but in the side of a mountain. He whirled and stared up at the mass of volcanic rock, then back at the forest, then up at the blue sky—blue sky with... His breath hitched. Two suns shone down on him from the sky. Two! He held out his hands, feeling the heat of the suns warm his bare skin. What. The. Fuck?

Another large, prehistoric-looking bird flew over-head. He stumbled backward, craning his neck to get a better look.

"He won't hurt you. That's my cousin." Charlotte leaned against the entry to the veranda, the feathers of her wings fluttering in a warm breeze that drifted up, smelling oddly of orange blossoms. "I'm sure Harlow or Marius will be along in just a moment."

"Who is—?"

A roar, loud as a jet engine, rumbled through his bones, and Liam whirled to see a massive gold *dragon* the size of a Boeing headed straight for him. He staggered backward into the room, hit his ass on a chair, and almost flipped over it. He gripped the back to steady himself.

"Are you okay?" Charlotte appeared in front of him. She glanced at a small kitchenette at the back of the room. "Would you like some water?"

"Dra-dragon." He wasn't prone to stuttering, but he was having an awful time forming words at the moment.

"Yes. Sorry. I should have warned you. Paragon is a dragon kingdom. That was my Aunt Harlow. She shifts to look like you or me. You just caught her giving her whelps a flying lesson."

His mouth formed into an *o*, but no sound came out. Eventually pure curiosity overrode his paralyzing fear, and one foot in front of the other, he strode onto the balcony again. For a few minutes he soaked it all in, using his analytical mind to suspend the rising terror in his chest and simply observe. This was no abduction by a Russian oligarch's daughter in cosplay. Charlotte wasn't lying. A different world lay before him, waiting to be discovered. He had no idea how this was all possible, but it was. Liam was on another planet.

Although terror was evident in every strained beat of his heart, Liam began to feel something else as he braced himself on the railing. A rush of excitement barreled through him, the same unparalleled intellectual delight he'd first experienced when he learned about dinosaurs as a boy, or during his first chemistry experiment. Sheer wonder trumped every other thought and reaction. Were the elements the same here? Was he the first human to ever visit Paragon? He could breathe the air—that was something. What would he find if he looked at the soil under a microscope? What kind of creature was this angel and the dragons she called family?

Everything about this situation frightened him. Everything about it excited him too. Heart thumping in his chest, he wondered if this was how Neil Armstrong felt before his first steps on the moon.

"Would you like me to take you back now?" Charlotte said from behind him, her wings drooping sadly in conjunction with the corners of her mouth. "I think I'm rested enough. I can do it."

"First tell me why you brought me here?" he said gruffly. He hadn't meant for the words to come out as harsh as they had, but he was not a man given to gentle speech.

She jolted at his tone. "As I explained before, I made a mistake. I was told that Saint Nick would be at Earth's North Pole, wearing a red suit. I thought you were him. I asked you if you would help me and you said yes, and so I brought you here, thinking you were him. I had no idea he was fictional."

He grunted disapprovingly. "I followed your explanation. What I want to know is what kind of help did you want from Santa?"

Heaving a heavy sigh, she said, "I need to throw a Christmas, and I don't know how to do it."

He squinted at her incredulously. Had he heard her correctly? "Throw... a... Christmas?"

"My aunt Avery is going through a hard time right now. She's originally from Earth and mentioned wanting to be home for Christmas, but the, uh, procedure she's having means she's going to miss it. I want to surprise her with a Christmas here. I want a party waiting for her when she returns from her trip."

Liam's curious mind didn't know where to start with all the questions he had following that explanation. If her aunt was from Earth, she must be human. How was Charlotte an angel? And where was Paragon in the universe? How had they traveled here?

All his thoughts narrowed to a single truth. He had a responsibility—no, a *duty*—to the scientific community to learn more about this strange and fascinating place. "I may not be Santa Claus, but I can help you with your Christmas party." After all, he'd celebrated Christmas every year of his life. Sure, he hadn't actually ever organized a holiday—his mom had always taken care of that—but how hard could it be?

"You can?"

"I'm from Earth. I know all about Christmas." He

rested his hands on his hips, his gaze drifting to the volcanic rock under the balcony. Interesting.

"But, I mean, will you? You sounded angry about the situation a moment ago." She crossed her arms. "I don't want you to think you don't have a choice. It was a simple misunderstanding."

He stormed toward her, making full use of his superior height. He needed to understand her position in this world. Was she military? A scientist? "Who are you here?"

Her gaze flicked down to her hands like a chastised child. Definitely not military. "You mean what is my title?" When he nodded, she said, "I am the princess of Paragon."

Hmm. Political then. "Well, *Princess*, you abducted me from my work. I bear part of the responsibility for that because I did agree to help you, only I assumed the help you needed would take place on my world. But now that I'm here, I think we can come to an agreement. First tell me the truth about how we got here."

"We, uh…" She straightened, and when she spoke again, her voice was terse. "As I said earlier, I can dimension walk. I leaped between worlds and brought you back with me."

"And you say you can return me when we are through."

"I can, but…" She hesitated. "You should know that time flows unevenly between here and there and I can only control when I land to a certain degree."

He blinked against a brewing headache. "Did you just say that time here flows at a different rate than Earth?"

She nodded. "Like two rivers running parallel to each other, each flowing at a different rate of speed. I can jump between one and the other, and with my magic, I can navigate to the same spot I left. But the longer you stay here, the harder it will be for you to adjust to the time shift. You might live a week here and have to relive that same week on Earth. It's disorienting to some."

He thought about that for a second. If she was lying and couldn't time travel—Jesus, was he even considering the idea that she could?—Noah would be long gone. Oh, he'd have searched for him and upon not finding his body would have assumed he'd slipped through the ice or met another untimely end. If she returned him to the place he left, he might be stuck there without a crew and no way off the ice. "Later, when you return me, if there's a problem, can you transport me to my home in Chicago rather than the North Pole?"

Her eyes widened. "Oh yes. I have an aunt and uncle who live in Chicago. My aunt is head of the vampire coven there."

Liam leaned harder against the chair behind him. "Vampire coven?"

"Oh, I forgot vampires aren't known to all humans, are they? Let's just say I can easily return you to Chicago and I have help there if we run into any issues with our jump. I've never actually been there, but it shouldn't be difficult."

Charlotte took a step toward him, that time-stopping smile returning to her face. A flutter of excitement started in his stomach, and he told himself it was about this new adventure and not attraction to this woman... this *creature*. He repeated the notion to himself as his gaze lingered on her mouth.

An incredible new world lay before him, a gorgeous princess with wings he was itching to examine if she'd let him, and his biggest risk of staying was missing some time from Earth and his crew assuming he died? Sorry, Noah, but he wasn't going anywhere.

"I'll stay and I'll help you, *Princess*, on one condition."

"What's that?"

"I'm a scientist and I'm curious about your world. I'll expect you to answer my questions when I ask." Liam stared her down, hands still on his hips.

"Deal." Her wings lifted slightly. Fascinating how he could read her mood by their position.

After a beat of silence as he contemplated where to start, he scowled when he realized he was dressed in only his base layer. "And I'll need appropriate clothing."

FIVE

The first time Charlie had seen Liam, she'd thought he looked like a bear. She hadn't expected he'd also have the personality of one. The man never smiled, spoke as if he was barking at her, and was about as warm as the sheet of ice she'd retrieved him from. In fact, there seemed to be a permanent crease in his brow.

Based on his disposition, she might have concluded all human men had terrible tempers except her uncle Nick, Rowan's mate, was human and wasn't anything like the grumpy Liam. Which left her with no choice but to assume that he was the problem. Oh well, he'd promised to help her with the Christmas. That's what she wanted after all. Did it matter how much he snapped? He wasn't a pet she meant to keep.

At least he wasn't hard to look at. She might have enjoyed carting him around the kingdom in the clingy red outfit he'd arrived in, but alas, she'd given into his demands and found him something to wear thanks to Uncle Alexander, who'd kept his clothing from his time on Earth. Alexander hadn't exactly reacted positively to her introduction of Liam and their situation, but he'd agreed to help her nonetheless. Only now, as they stood outside the bathroom in his chambers waiting for Liam to finish changing, his foot tapped like the tail of an annoyed cat.

"Is something wrong, Uncle?"

He scratched the back of his head. "Are you sure about this, Charlie? I don't think Raven and Gabriel would like you jumping dimensions without their permission. And bringing a hapless human here? You've made better choices, kiddo."

Chewing her lip, she bristled at the "kiddo" epithet. She was no child. Still, he was right about one thing—she hadn't considered that her parents might believe Liam was a security risk. "It was an innocent mistake. I was going off what I'd read in the book—"

"I can appreciate that. North Pole, red suit, beard. Anyone might have made the same error. That part is reasonable. What I don't understand is why he's still here."

"He volunteered to stay. He said he knows a lot about Christmas and is willing to help me."

A low rumble vibrated from her uncle's chest. "What do you really know about this human?"

"Practically nothing. He's a human scientist who was studying ice at the North Pole. That's about it."

"Then how do you know you can trust him?"

She scoffed. "He's helping me throw an Earth Christmas-themed party, not counting the palace's dragmars." She turned to face him, folding her arms. "Are you questioning my ability to manage a hapless human?"

He released a sigh. "Don't get me wrong, Charlie—I think Avery will appreciate the party, and I think it will show Raven you have the skills to organize something big."

"But?"

"But you brought a stranger into the palace without permission." Alexander tugged on his ear as if this entire situation was making him twitch.

"You're right. I did. And if he was dangerous in any way, I'd consider it a poor choice on my part. But he's just a human. I could split him in half with a single blast from my hand." Flipping one hand over, palm up, she allowed her power to dance across her palm, a tiny electrical storm. "I won't let him out of my sight."

"But, uh, Charlie, there's more to this than that." Alexander shifted uneasily.

"I'll wipe his mind before I take him back to Earth, okay? There's nothing to worry about, Uncle."

He frowned. "What about while he's here? Where do you plan to have him *sleep*?"

She spread her hands. Where was he going with this? What were the options? "My chambers."

His head shook vehemently. "No. I am not comfortable with that. At all." Alexander lowered his voice. "What if he attempts to take advantage of you?"

The whirling ball of lightning in her palm returned and grew larger with her rising anger. "Let's find out. Pretend you're him."

Alexander stepped back. Celestial magic was one of the few things that could actually burn a dragon. It could positively cremate a human. And she controlled a sizable amount of it.

"Point taken." Alexander held up his hands and laughed, then rubbed his stubbled jaw. "You can take care of yourself. Only..."

"Yes?"

"What will other people think?"

She squinted at him, flicking her hand and reabsorbing the magic. "Sorry?"

"You have your reputation to consider. Your... marriageability as a princess."

She snorted, turning to lean against the back of his sofa and crossing her arms. "Seriously? Uncle, I can confidently say I'm in no danger of losing marriage prospects. None exist to lose."

He sighed heavily. "For now, but in the future—"

"The future holds no further prospects. No male in this kingdom wants a wife who can melt the skin from his body."

"Gabriel would kill me if I allowed you to compromise yourself."

So that was it. Charlie fluffed her wings. "I love you, Uncle, but I'm doing this. I will handle it. I promise you, nothing will happen with this human and I will be discreet about his time here. I will put him in my second bedroom and take care to keep my distance in public."

Uncle Alexander sighed but nodded his head. "Good plan. I trust you to stay out of trouble. And keep him out of trouble too." Alexander left her side to cross to his bar and pour a glass of amber-colored liquor.

"There's a simple solution for that. If he causes trouble, I'll take him back to Earth."

He returned to her side, pointing a finger at the bathroom door. "Just make sure I get my clothes back before you do. Those are some of my favorite mementos from my time in Sedona."

Charlie laughed. Uncle Alexander loved his old Earth clothes. As a dragon, he was far bigger than Liam now, but there was a time before his mate Maiara was resurrected when he'd starved himself to the size of a human. Liam was somewhere between those two sizes, closer to her uncle now than back then. Luckily, Alexander had several options and had sent Liam into the bathroom with a stack and a few different pairs of boots.

"Deal." She bumped shoulders with her uncle. "He

goes back in the red suit or what he was wearing under it. I promise."

"Good. And, um, Charlie?"

"Yeah?"

"If your dad asks, I don't know anything about him staying in your rooms. Not a thing. I plead total ignorance."

"Fair enough." She gave him a consoling smile. Charlie had no intention of doing anything inappropriate with the grumpy and hairy man she'd brought back from Earth. All she wanted was the information that was in his head. She was young by dragon standards, and she could appreciate her uncle's perspective, but there was absolutely no attraction on her part to—

The door to the bathroom opened, and Charlie's thoughts scattered like frightened mice. The man standing in front of her looked nothing like the rumpled, scraggly creature she'd dragged from the puffy red suit and lugged to her bed. He'd combed his mess of hair and trimmed the unruly beard, revealing a sharp jawline and pleasantly full lips. With his dark hair tamed, his intense gaze met hers from under impossibly thick lashes, his eyes the color of polished amber and bright as if lit from within.

He ran a hand down the black T-shirt he was wearing—it clung like it was enjoying the taste of him —and eyed Alexander's modern Paragonian garb. "Will this do, or will I look like an earthling?"

"Earthling." Alexander chuckled. "That's funny."

"We just call you humans," Charlie said. "And you look fine. Anyway, no matter what you wear, people will know you're human."

"Oh."

"You're smaller and you have no wings or markings. Plus there's your smell."

His lips parted as if he was going to say something but couldn't find the words.

"Just stick with Charlie and nothing will eat you," Alexander said with a snort.

Liam scowled and looked in her direction. "He's joking, right?"

Oddly, Charlie's tongue felt unusually large in her mouth when he looked at her. She had to clear her throat a few times to loosen it. "Nothing is going to eat you," she said through a cheerful grin. "As long as we stay away from the vampires of Nochtbend and don't anger any dragons, you'll be fine."

A low grunt came from Liam's throat. "Vampires... right. Here too, eh? Not just in Chicago?"

"They mostly keep to the kingdom of Nochtbend. And they sleep during the day. We might not even see one." She waved a hand in the air dismissively. It was really nothing to worry about. No vampire would bother Liam with her around. Although he didn't look happy about the situation. Oh well, he'd agreed to help her, and that was what was important. She'd spent enough time among dragons to be immune to his sour personality.

Alexander took a sip of his drink. "I need to get back to work. Where do you two plan to start?" He glared pointedly at Liam.

Few men could hold their own on the receiving end of a dragon's stare. Alexander's eyes were filled with fire, and the grit in his voice told her his question held a tinge of a threat. He didn't trust Liam, or maybe he didn't trust any man around Charlie. But Liam seemed unbothered.

He glared at her uncle and said, "We need an evergreen tree and a place to put it."

"I'll take him to Everfield," Charlie said.

Alexander nodded, then stepped forward to grip Liam's biceps, bringing his face close to the human's. "Good. Find the tree, plan the party, and stay out of trouble. And remember, Princess Charlie is beloved by all, *human.*"

Liam held her uncle's stare with his own. "Got it," he gritted out.

Charlie swooped in and tugged Liam from her uncle's grip, ushering him toward the door. "Thanks, Uncle Alex! I owe you one."

LESS THAN AN HOUR LATER, CHARLIE WAS BUMPING ALONG the road to Everfield in a royal carriage, Liam on the seat across from her. She'd sent a falcon ahead to Uncle Sylas and Aunt Dianthe, informing them that she was coming to the kingdom of the fairies and might need their help in finding a proper tree. There were only two places on Ouros with evergreen trees: Darnuith and Everfield. Collecting one from Darnuith was out of the question. Wards around the kingdom would alert Queen Penelope to her presence immediately, potentially interrupt the spell they'd be performing, and completely ruin the surprise. The Empyrean Wood in Everfield, however, claimed to contain every type of tree in their world and beyond, and with Dianthe's help, she was sure they'd find the perfect one.

The carriage lurched to a halt.

"Why are we stopping?" Liam's hands were planted firmly on his thighs, his expression as humorless as ever.

"Just the border toll to Nochtbend. We'll resume in a moment."

"Nochtbend? The place with the vampires?" Liam pulled back the curtain on the window and peeked out at the misty edge of Grimtwist Forest.

"Don't worry," she said with a laugh. "The suns are still up. They're all asleep. Plus we're not stopping, just passing through to get to Everfield. Even if it were the middle of the night, few vampires would dare interfere with a royal carriage on a major roadway."

He leaned against the velvet seat and rested his

ankle on his knee. "That's right—the princess is beloved by all."

She didn't care for the disdainful tone of his voice. "Does it bother you that I'm a princess?"

"Only so much as it attracts threats from men like your uncle. You brought me here. I don't appreciate being treated like I've got a gun to your head."

She folded her arms. "Are all scientists on Earth as irritable as you?"

His brows shot up. "Irritable? You think I'm overreacting to the circumstances?"

"No." She crossed her legs, her foot bobbing between them. Were scientists held in high esteem on Earth? What was their relative position in society? It was possible her title made him uncomfortable if he came from a lower caste. She tried to be empathetic as she responded. "I apologize on behalf of my uncle. He means well and he loves me, but that doesn't give him the right to intimidate you."

His only response was one curt nod, his eyes fixated on the window. Silence slid between them in the carriage, the only sound the clip-clop of the mountain horse's hooves. She was relieved when he finally turned his face back to her.

"Do you enjoy being a princess?"

"No one has ever asked me that before."

"First time for everything."

She studied Liam's face as she considered how to answer. A princess was simply what she was. She didn't have a choice. "I think so. My parents run the kingdom for all intents and purposes. To be honest, I have few responsibilities for which I'm solely account-able. That's part of the reason I wanted to throw this party. I want to prove to them that they can trust me with more."

Casually, he uncrossed his ankles and stretched his legs toward her. "Seriously? You seem capable enough to me. Fuck, you jumped worlds into one of the harshest environments on Earth to bring me here. I'd say you're a woman who can get things done."

She smiled. "Thank you for that."

"Which part?"

"All of it. But especially calling me a woman. My family still treats me like a child."

"I gathered that when your uncle got in my face. How old are you anyway?"

"That's a harder question to answer than you might think. By your timeline, I am twenty-five."

"By my timeline? Do you mean because of the difference in the pace of time between our worlds?"

She tucked her hair behind her ears. "Uh, no, although that's a factor as well. From the time I was born, I aged faster than a human child. When I was two Earth years old, I both appeared and had the intel-lectual maturity of a ten-year-old. I stopped aging when I reached this size and appearance, about ten years ago."

"Full-grown at fifteen?"

She nodded. "I am an adult both by your standards and ours. Do you mind me asking...?" She gestured at him.

"Thirty-eight... in human years." He didn't exactly smile, but his eyes tightened at the corners as if he was tempted. "So your parents... You said they treat you like a child. They don't include you in royal matters?"

"Oh, they include me, but it's like I'm a marble statue they park in the room. I don't lead anything, and my assignments are few and usually nonessential."

"Hmm. Difficult. No wonder you wanted to throw this party. Probably bored out of your head."

She was bored for a number of reasons, but she felt uncomfortable diving deeper into it with this stranger, so she smiled and turned the tables on the conversation. "What about you? Are you happy being a scientist?"

His brows lifted. "Not sure anyone's asked me that before."

"First time for everything."

"I love it even when I'm obtaining a sample of ice by the light of the moon in Arctic temperatures." He picked at the side of his thumbnail, silence coming between them again for a beat until he added, "You might say I gave up being a prince to do it."

What? Leaning forward, she lowered her voice. "You were once a human prince?"

He groaned. "In a sense. My grandparents founded

Morrismart. My family is the closest thing to American royalty there is."

"What's Morrismart?" she probed, even more curious about this stranger. If he'd once been the equivalent of a prince, why had he seemed put off by her role as princess?

"It's this gigantic retail store that sells everything from kayaks to greeting cards. My father was a genius when it came to logistics, so he developed software that not only finds the cheapest price but also the cheapest way to get items to our warehouse. He invented a groundbreaking predictive model for what and how much to order as well."

She tried to picture such a store and couldn't. Stores like that did not exist in Paragon. The concept sounded overwhelming. "And this makes you a prince?"

"My family's collective wealth makes us the third wealthiest in America and the fifteenth wealthiest in the world."

"You must be so proud." Although she tried to keep her expression neutral, Liam was beginning to sound like some of the men who'd come sniffing around the castle, only interested in marrying a princess for how she might elevate their position.

To her surprise though, he shook his head. "No... not at all. Morrismart is a plague on the planet. The company sells mass amounts of cheap, single-use plastics that end up in the landfills or our oceans. And don't get me started about where the products come from. The labor practices are awful. It's why I refused to be a part of it. Instead, I earned my PhD, eschewed my inheritance, and became an environmental scientist. Not only did I leave the company behind, my research has led to new regulations that are forcing them to make changes for the better. They hate that, by the way."

Fascinating. Charlie wasn't expecting that. Most men she'd met were at least partially interested in her fortune and always interested in preserving their own. "You left all the money behind?"

He shifted as if the question made him uncomfortable. "Yes. Believe me, when I think what that money could do for the planet, I sometimes wonder if I've done the right thing. But my inheritance came with a stipulation that I work for the company, so it was a no-go for me. Unfortunately, my income as a professor is barely enough for a one-bedroom efficiency in Chicago." He frowned. "Does it bother you that you reached for a celestial being and nabbed a broke PhD instead?"

"Why would it bother me?" When he didn't answer right away, she studied him a moment longer and then it dawned on her. Did he think his lower economic status made him unworthy for her task? Or —and she hated to presume this because there was far too much wishful thinking involved—was he considering himself as her possible match and wondering if wealth was important to her? Either way, there was only one answer to give. "No. It doesn't bother me. I think the choices you've made are admirable. Was it a difficult transition for you?"

"Not really." He turned his head to look out the window, getting a far-off look in his eye. "Occasionally I miss how it was before, being a family."

She wanted to ask him more about that, but the carriage lurched to a stop and the driver opened the door for them. She'd barely stepped off the bottom step when she was swept into her uncle Sylas's arms.

Liam was highly motivated to make a good impression on yet another uncle after Alex's threat. This uncle was even bigger than the last, although he'd never thought it possible, and the man —er, dragon—had a chilling gleam in his gunmetal-gray eyes. No doubt this would be the dragon who would chew him up, bones and all, if he stepped out of line.

"Uncle Sylas, this is my friend Liam from Earth. He's helping me."

"It's a pleasure to meet you." Liam held out a hand congenially. The dragon studied it for a moment, then shook it awkwardly. "I'm sensing that shaking hands isn't a common gesture here."

Sylas shook his head slowly. "Welcome to Everfield." His gaze slid back to Charlotte. "Dianthe's going to meet us at the house. She had a little mishap with one of the kids."

"Oh? What happened this time?" Charlotte laughed.

Groaning, Sylas glanced up at the cloudless sky. "Annabelle met a boy, and Dianthe caught them alone in her room."

"Uh-oh." Charlotte bobbed her eyebrows. "I guess she *is* fifteen."

"Don't remind me."

Although Sylas had suggested he was taking them to his home, the dragon led them straight into the woods from the road. Liam wondered if this was some kind of shortcut. Lucky break—he couldn't get enough of the surrounding flora, which was unlike anything he'd ever seen before. Some of the trees looked like something out of a Dr. Seuss picture book. The colors, the shapes... They shouldn't exist.

Not everything was foreign. He recognized members of the oak, maple, sycamore, and hawthorn families, although the trees weren't exactly representative of their earthly counterparts. Trunks that were normally straight in the species were twisted and knotted. Leaves had unexpected indentations. He took it all in, studying each plant until he'd fallen behind.

"I need paper and something to sketch with," he demanded, stopping short to examine a fern with bright orange tentacles that waved at him from its shady home.

Charlotte dropped back to his side. "Okay. We don't have time to stop now though. Can you wait until we're back at the palace?"

He was suddenly very thankful for his eidetic memory. "Yeah. That'll work."

They started walking again, and this time she matched his pace. "My aunt and uncle adopted nine children."

"Nine?" Liam felt his brows creep toward his hairline. He was the oldest of three, and sometimes that felt like too many siblings.

"They can't have children of their own, so a few years back they decided to adopt and give as many orphans a home as possible. Now they have Annabelle, Lilly, Dash, Rose, Hyacinth, Ash, Nigella, Reed, and Wren. I don't remember all their ages, but Annabelle just turned fifteen and there's a year or two between each one, ending with the youngest, Wren, who is five."

"Wow, nine kids. That's commitment."

She giggled. "It's uncommon here, but I think because Sylas came from a family of nine—"

"You have eight uncles?" Liam's voice cracked. Eight uncles and a dragon dad as big and as bad. If he'd been afraid to slip up before, he was nine times as afraid now.

"Seven uncles and one aunt, although it's my aunt Rowan people are the most afraid of. She's smaller but as clever as dragons come. She lives in New York with her human mate, Nick."

Weirdly, his heart gave an unexpected squeeze at that information. "She has a human mate?"

Charlotte shot him a coy smile. "Yes. She owns an art gallery there. He used to be a detective, but he's retired now." She looked away, and he got the sense that she'd been about to say something more.

A cacophony of voices called their attention to a cottage straight out of a fairy tale and beyond anything Liam could've imagined. It resembled a human house only in the sense that there was a roof, a door, and windows. The rest was something from a dream. Branches of the tree the home was built into formed its walls—living branches that continued growing toward Paragon's two suns beyond the home's exterior. It was a proper tree house with a trunk that was wider than he was tall and a front stoop that hovered a good twenty feet off the ground. But the most incredible part was the smoke billowing from a stone chimney. By some miracle or magic, this living tree house had a fireplace.

"I'll fly him up," Sylas offered, wings sprouting from his back.

Liam jolted backward. Those bat-like wings had talons longer than his head at their apex!

"I have him," Charlotte said mercifully. Before he could say another word, her arms wrapped around him and the scent of sunlight, citrus, and new grass filled his nose. He wouldn't have thought that scent existed before her, but here it was, warm and fragrant. She was spring and life and—

His feet lifted off the ground, the beat of her wings creating a soft thump, thump in the air around him. Charlie landed with a thud and released him once they reached the threshold.

He straightened his T-shirt. "Um, thanks."

She nodded, then followed her uncle into the cottage. Winged children buzzed around the home like bees in a hive. He marveled at their complexions of every color. Not colors of people like on Earth. Actual *colors*—lavender, pink, lime, and saffron—every color of the rainbow. He couldn't help but laugh in wonder at the absurdity of their existence. This couldn't be real.

"Aunt Charlie!" A half dozen small fairies rushed into her arms, and Liam caught himself smiling as he watched her lift the smallest one and swing her around in a circle. "We missed you!" they said in unison.

"I missed you all too."

"Are you here to watch us?" A winged-girl with turquoise skin bounced on her toes as she clung to Charlotte's arm.

"Not today, Nig." She kissed the girl's head tenderly, and Liam frowned at the warm tightness it caused inside his chest. The sense of family it evoked had become foreign to him the past few years.

"Who is this guest of my niece?" An adult fairy entered the room, her color deeper than the others. She might have passed as a black woman among humans if not for the pair of gold butterfly-like wings spreading from her back.

"This is my friend Liam," Charlotte said.

Sylas approached the black woman and kissed her soundly on the lips. "Liam, this is my mate, Dianthe. She knows the Empyrean Wood better than any being alive. She's going to help you."

After the look Sylas had given him, he refrained from extending his hand but gave her a nod of acknowledgment. "I'd appreciate the help."

"What is he, Mama?" the small turquoise fairy asked, having left Charlotte's side to stand directly in front of him. Her oversized green eyes blinked curiously in his direction.

"That's a human like Uncle Nick, Nigella," Dianthe explained.

"Oh. He looks stupid and he smells funny."

"Nigella! That's not nice." Charlotte chastised the girl, and Dianthe and Sylas chimed in their disapproval.

"Well, his mouth is hanging open!" Nigella protested, pointing her finger at him.

Liam deliberately closed his mouth, which *had* dropped open, and straightened, trying to play it cool.

"He's adjusting. He's never seen fairies before," Charlotte said.

Thinking fast, he cleared his throat and said, "Nigella, maybe you can teach me something about fairies. What is your favorite thing to do when you have free time?"

"I like to collect pollen from the sunpitchers in Solaris Field," she said enthusiastically.

"Oh, that does sound fun." He had no idea what collecting pollen entailed, but he kept his voice light as he asked, "What do you do with it once you collect it?"

Nigella's head rolled back on her neck, and she gave him a wide smile that was missing two front teeth. "You eat it, silly!"

Sylas's hand landed on top of Nigella's head. "That's enough. Go pick up your room. It's a disaster in there." After the child flew off toward the back of the cottage, Sylas said, "Sorry about that. They have no filter at that age."

Liam gave a gritty laugh. "My sister is thirty-six and still doesn't have one."

Thankfully, Sylas seemed to get his humor because he laughed too. "I have a sister like that."

"Rowan," he said.

"You know her?"

"Not personally. Charlotte was just telling me about her in the carriage."

The entire room went silent, and Dianthe's eyes drifted to the angel by his side, a tight, twitchy smile on her lips. "Oh... *Charlotte* told you about her, did she?"

Liam glanced back to see his new friend's cheeks burning bright red. He hadn't meant to embarrass her by calling her by her full name. It just suited her better. Charlie sounded young and simple. The angel in front of him was more than that. She deserved to be called a sophisticate name. Damn if that blush didn't do something to his insides though. He looked away before his body could respond to the raw tingle that had taken up residence in his veins.

"I hear you're looking for an evergreen tree," Dianthe said, breaking the tension in the room.

"Yes," he said, trying his best to take on an air of confidence and professionalism. He could handle this. He needed to handle this. "Usually a Christmas tree is triangular in shape and coniferous, meaning—"

"I know what coniferous means!" Dianthe said with some offense. "I'm a fairy. We know our trees like we know our own limbs, and we have specimens here from your world thanks to our friends from Earth. Come, I think I know what you're looking for."

Sylas caught a child out of the air and tossed him over his shoulder where he giggled and squirmed. "I'll feed the crew while you're gone."

"There're honey cakes in the kitchen," Dianthe said.

Cheers rose up from every corner, and winged children Liam hadn't noticed before appeared and ran for the next room.

"Be back soon, you guys. This shouldn't take long."

Dianthe walked to the threshold and launched herself into the air.

"Hang on tight," Charlotte whispered in his ear. She was pressed up against his back again, and the feel of her so close sent a pulse through him. "My aunt is fast as a hummingbird."

"Are we going to—?"

She gripped him from behind and launched herself off the threshold. His stomach dropped and lurched as she soared after her aunt, weaving between the trees at breakneck speed.

He clung to her, his feet dangling dangerously close to a sequoia as he pedaled them in the air. "Hey! I'd like to leave here someday with all my limbs."

She snorted in his ear. "Sorry. I'm not used to carrying someone as big and heavy as you."

Thank God. He was an inch or so taller than Charlotte, but it was hard not to feel emasculated when a woman whose figure was as graceful as a slender violin could toss you around like a child's toy. Liam was an athlete who'd spent months doing labor-intensive work in the Arctic and was big by human standards. Not sure why it was important to him, he was still glad she noticed.

Thankfully it wasn't long before Dianthe landed in a grove of coniferous trees beside a lake so blue it didn't seem real. Was he truly in a fairy tale? As his feet touched down on a carpet of dried needles, the intense smell of pine filled his lungs.

"My god, there's no place like this on Earth."

"You're not on Earth," Dianthe said through a smile. "Do you see anything like your Christmas tree?"

He came upon a yew tree and ran a hand along the branches. "We can cut pieces off this to decorate with. Humans hang them over doorways."

Dianthe pulled a bag from her belt and a pair of shears and handed them to Charlotte, who collected what he asked for. Around the next bend, he came across some holly, its shiny green leaves and red berries brighter than any he'd witnessed in a long time. "And this."

More greenery fell into the bag. Without knowing exactly how big the room was that Charlotte wanted him to decorate, it was hard to know how much to ask for, but he distracted himself from that thought almost immediately. Who cared if it was perfect? No one here knew what it was supposed to look like but him.

He strolled down the rows of trees: pines, firs, and something he was sure was a type of juniper lined the path, along with other coniferous specimens he didn't recognize at all. He took his time, inspecting each one and committing the details to memory. He almost forgot what he was supposed to be looking for until a perfectly proportioned spruce tree appeared in front of him, causing him to pull up short. If a flawless Christmas tree had ever existed, this was the one. The ideal height and width. Full all the way around.

"Is this it? Is this a Christmas tree?" Charlotte asked.

He sighed, a heavy pressure starting in his chest. He'd been warned by her uncles not to upset this angel he was supposed to be helping, but he was afraid he had no choice but to disappoint her today. "It is, but... I'm sorry, Charlotte, we can't use it."

Her brows knit together, and Liam had the strongest urge to kiss the space between her blue eyes. What the hell was wrong with him? Clearing his throat, he told her the truth. "This tree is perfect, but to get it back to the palace, we'd have to cut it down. It would be a crime to kill this tree. Not only does it appear to be the only spruce in this wood, it's got a long life ahead of it here. I won't be part of killing it just for your party. Believe me, this is one human tradition you don't want to bring to this planet."

He leaned back on his heels and hoped she'd let it go.

Behind him, Dianthe started to laugh. "Is that what you're worried about? Charlie, take your human back to the palace. We'll have the tree delivered by tomorrow afternoon."

"Oh hell no!" His jaw clenched. "You *can't* kill it. Truly, if you must have one, I'll build you an artificial one constructed of cut branches. Chopping down this tree would be criminal."

Dianthe walked away, shaking her head. "Nice to

see you again, Charlie. Say hello to everyone at the palace."

They waved goodbye to each other while Liam's head burned with his growing anger.

When Charlotte turned back to him, her smile faded. "She won't kill it, Liam! Trust me. No trees will die for this party."

He scowled. "Do you swear it?" Not something he'd usually ask his buddies, but this seemed like the type of place where people swore oaths and where promises stuck.

Charlotte linked her hand into his and started leading him away. "I swear it. Believe me, if fairies don't cut down trees to make their houses, they won't cut them down for a palace party."

"But then how—?"

Her gaze met his and held, her brow lifting slightly. "Trust me."

Odd. In the spotlight of those fathomless blue eyes, he did trust her. Warmth spread through his torso until he realized he was dangerously close to assigning feelings to the interaction. He blinked away the unwanted sensation and was relieved when the icy shield he used to protect his heart snapped back into place. Wow, what the hell was wrong with him? More curtly than he meant to, he snapped, "Fine," then strode in the direction of the carriage, breaking the spell she had over him.

SEVEN

Paragon's two moons had just peeked over the horizon as Charlie boarded the carriage again for home. Liam was already inside, having stormed ahead of her in a huff. She respected him for being the type of man who wouldn't kill a tree, but the dichotomy between that and his gruff personality gave her pause. Given that he was larger than the average human and had proven himself tough enough to face one of the most dangerous environments on Earth, it made sense that his nature was somewhat rugged and unrefined. She supposed he didn't have many people to talk to in his line of work after all. But his perpetually sour mood was beginning to grate on her.

Ah well, he wouldn't be here forever. She'd return him to earth in a few days and then she wouldn't have to deal with his gray cloud of a personality. And why did that particular reality make her heart feel heavy?

"Is something wrong?" she asked him once she was seated across from him and the carriage was in motion.

His eyes shifted to hers, his face impassive. "No."

She waited but he did not expound on his answer. Pursing her lips, she shifted in her seat, refusing to let his attitude dampen her spirits. They'd found a tree! She was well on her way to making this party happen. Straightening in her seat, she plastered a smile to her face and asked cheerfully, "What's next after the tree?"

Cracking his neck, he answered, "We'll need to decorate it. Stringed lights and multicolored glass balls usually, but anything shiny will do."

If there was one thing Paragon had no shortage of, it was shiny things. "I have some ideas. Then what?"

He sniffed, his jaw clenching as if he had to think hard about the question. "Cookies."

"I'll book some time in the kitchen tomorrow and you can show me how to make them."

He nodded, his mouth bending into a worried expression. "I'll, uh, have to try to remember the recipe. I usually have it in front of me."

"I'm sure we can figure it out. After the cookies?"

"Gifts. It's customary to choose a little something for each of your loved ones and wrap it in brightly colored paper."

"Oh, we definitely do gifts in Paragon. That part will be easy." She grinned.

He did not return her smile but stared at her and

sighed before adding flatly, "After that, it's just a matter of choosing what to make for the meal. I usually do ham. My parents usually do lobster or prime rib."

"You don't spend Christmas with your parents?"

"Only if I have to and only for the shortest amount of time necessary to meet my obligations."

Obligations. Charlie pitied him that. Even when they were in a disagreement, she never felt being in her parents' presence was an obligation. Was he truly not loved by his family?

"What exactly happened between you and them?" she asked softly. "I sensed before that there was more to your story."

He scoffed. "Like I said, we just have different values. They wanted me to fall in line working at Morrismart and I refused. I try my best to steer clear of them now." Liam's expression darkened just as the carriage lurched to a stop. "Is that the border crossing again?"

She shook her head. "It's after sunset, so we shouldn't have to stop." Charlie pulled the drapes aside to peek out the window and then rolled her eyes. They were in Nochtbend all right, but it wasn't the checkpoint that had stopped them.

The door flew open, and a vampire with hair the color of ripe wheat and eyes so pale they shone like diamonds in the night stood outside the carriage. She inwardly groaned. It was Prince Cassius, her ex-boyfriend and

Master Demidicus's new second-in-command. He was also the vampire she'd lost her virginity to. Her cheeks warmed at the memory. They'd parted on amiable terms, but he was the last person she wanted to see tonight.

"Cassius," she said, bowing her head slightly in his direction.

"Princess Charlie," he said with a swagger. "You weren't going to pass through Nochtbend without saying hello, were you?"

She coupled her hands at her waist. "My apologies. We are due back at the palace within the hour. I'm afraid I don't have time for a visit."

Long fingers extend toward her into the carriage, his sharp, overlong nails glinting in the moonlight. "Nonsense. Come, my dear. We have a fire nearby. Have a visit with your old friend."

Charlie's eyes darted to Liam. Until that moment, Cassius hadn't seemed to notice the human was there —he was too focused on Charlie. But when her gaze shifted, so did his attention. He sniffed the air and turned to face her guest.

"What have we here?" Cassius's eyes blazed with curiosity.

"Cassius, this is Liam. He's a guest of the palace. My guest." By stressing the last part, Charlie hoped to convey ownership to Cassius, vampire language that amounted to a warning for him to control that hint of hunger she saw in his eyes. He wasn't a bad vampire, and Charlie had never felt unsafe around him, but any vampire could be unpredictable. Her parents had taught her that.

"Liam, you don't mind delaying your trip to enhance diplomatic relations, do you?" Cassius said through a broad smile.

Liam's face was hidden in shadow, but he leaned forward into the strip of moonlight that filtered through the open door, seeming to fill the carriage with the breadth of his shoulders. He did not return Cassius's smile as he responded, "I believe Charlotte just said we need to return directly to the palace."

Cassius scoffed. "Ah, but that was before the kingdom of Nochtbend extended an invitation to the princess of Paragon. It would be quite rude for her to deny me now."

Liam glared at Cassius, his eyes never leaving the vampire's face as he asked, "That true, Charlotte?"

Cassius turned back to Charlie, his smile growing impossibly wider, packed with too many teeth. "Please, *Charlotte*, for old times' sake. Half the court is around the fire. They've seen the royal carriage. Do your royal duty and say hello."

She sighed. Refusing him now that he'd suggested the group in question were Nochtbend dignitaries could be viewed as a political offense. She put her hand on Liam's. "I should go. You can wait here if you like."

"I go where you go," he said in a low, gritty timbre, his eyes still fixed on Cassius.

The vampire backed away from the door, his arms spreading wide. "Then welcome, guests. Follow me."

Charlie stepped down from the carriage, then turned back toward Liam. "Can you see in the dark?"

"Not without a set of night vision goggles."

"What are night vision goggles?"

He shook his head. "No. I can't see in the dark."

She allowed her inner light to shine as she had the first night they'd met and watched his amber eyes blink rapidly against her glow.

"Beautiful," he murmured.

She tucked her hair behind her ear and flashed him a crooked smile. "Thanks."

"This way," Cassius called from up ahead.

She slipped her hand into Liam's and whispered, "Stay with me. It will be fine."

"I plan to stay with you, fine or otherwise." His already somber expression turned darker.

The crackle of the fire greeted them up ahead. Cassius wasn't lying. Charlie recognized several young dignitaries from the Nochtbend coven, snuggled with their dates around the fire. They all stood when they saw her and bowed, greetings of "Princess Charlie" reaching her through the darkness.

Cassius sat down on a log opposite the fire and patted the space beside him. He didn't seem to have a date tonight, which concerned her. She hoped he didn't intend to put her in the position of acting in that role. To be polite, she sat beside him but pulled Liam down on her other side, keeping hold of his hand.

"What's the cause for celebration tonight?" she asked.

Cassius wrapped an arm around her shoulders, ignoring her and Liam's coupled hands. She shifted in Liam's direction, putting some distance between her and the vampire, but Cassius simply leaned closer.

"Metluk and Andromeda were officially mated this dusk." He gestured to a couple to their left. "We've just come from the celebratory feast to play the traditional mating games."

"I'm not familiar with this ritual. What type of games do you play?" she asked.

Metluk lifted a chalice from the ground near his feet. "Actually, it's fortuitous that you've joined us, Charlie. Cassius doesn't have a date, and this game is usually played by couples."

She stiffened. Exactly what she'd been afraid of.

"He still doesn't have a date," Liam gritted out in a voice as low as a mountain bear's growl.

The others laughed, but Charlie felt Cass stiffen beside her. It wouldn't do to anger him. The last thing she wanted was to put Liam in danger. She had to distract Cass from the comment and from Liam. "How is the game played?"

Cassius removed his arm from her shoulders and

clapped his hands together. "It's called risk or ruse. We go around the fire and each person chooses to either perform a physical feat or tell a story, true or untrue, about a topic of the asker's choosing. If the story is found to be untrue, the participant must do the physical challenge instead."

Liam's snort cut through the darkness. "Like truth or dare."

"What's that?" Charlie asked.

"Never mind," he mumbled. "Just things aren't as different here as I thought."

"One round," Charlie said, "and then we really must be going. My driver is waiting."

"Oh fine. If you must. One round then," Cassius said. "Metluk, you first. I'll start the asking."

"Risk!" Metluk announced, puffing out his chest and giving Andromeda a wink.

Cassius glanced in Liam's direction, his gaze locking with the human's as he said, "Stick your hand in the fire for fifteen seconds."

Metluk flipped him off. "You're an asshole, Cass."

Cassius turned back to his friend and shrugged. "If you weren't prepared for a challenge, you should have picked ruse."

The vampire growled but stuck his hand into the flames, glaring at Cassius as he did so. Charlie winced at the smell of burning hair and then flesh as the other vampires counted down from fifteen. She was relieved when Metluk finally met the challenge and yanked his charred hand from the fire. Reaching for the chalice near his feet, he drank deeply of the contents. Each of the vampires had a similar cup, and she supposed it was filled with blood by the way his arm was already healing.

"This is fucking insane," Liam grumbled beside her.

She squeezed his hand supportively.

"Andromeda, risk or ruse?" Elsa asked, her bright red hair shining in the firelight from her place on Cass's other side.

"Ruse," she responded.

"Tell us about a moment you questioned your relationship with Metluk."

She shrugged, her fangs extending as she answered quickly. "Easy. The last night I spent with his cousin and her mate. It will be difficult to give up group sex now that we're mated."

Metluk hissed and glared at her protectively.

"Her answer is true," Elsa said through a laugh.

Next in line was Cassius, and he looked across the circle to Valcrun before stating "ruse" in a loud, clear voice.

"Coward!" Metluk snapped.

"Admittedly so," Cassius said proudly.

Valcrun glanced around the group, shadows from the crackling fire dancing over his face and giving him a demonic appearance. He smiled wickedly before asking, "When you had Princess Charlie in your bed, how did you manage the wings?"

All the vampires burst into laughter, but ice filled Charlie's veins so thoroughly it began to snow around her. The crackle of her power danced across her skin, and she felt the burn as her eyes filled with the same celestial magic.

"Don't answer that," Liam barked at Cassius.

"What's that, human?" Cassius grinned wickedly.

Liam stood, his overall size dwarfing any of the vampires around the fire. "I said shut the fuck up about it. It's no one's business but yours and hers."

"Ooh hoo hoo hoo!" Valcrun said. "He's feisty. Fine. I retract my question if for no other reason than Charlie's mood might douse the fire." He held out his hand to catch one of the snowflakes she was putting off.

She took a deep breath and the snow stopped falling, although a few flakes had already built up on Liam's shoulders. She tugged his hand, and he sat down again.

Valcrun cleared his throat. "Instead, you may answer this. What position do you aspire to on the Nochtbend court?"

Cassius swatted the air with one hand. "A gentle toss of a question, Valcrun. You're going soft. I aspire to no less than becoming master, as most vampires do."

"True," Valcrun said. "Princess Charlie, you're up."

"Risk," Charlie said. It was her safest bet. Her celestial magic made her practically invulnerable, and she didn't want to be asked about her romantic history with Cassius.

Sabine shifted on her log, her keen eyes studying her and Liam. After a few quiet moments, she lowered her chin and shot her a wicked grin. "Kiss your human guest."

"What?" Charlie asked breathlessly, her cheeks growing hot. She'd only just met the human that day. She glanced in Liam's direction. He was scowling, like always. His face hadn't cracked a smile since his arrival.

"Kiss him." Sabine gestured toward Liam. "Oh, come now, it's just a kiss. I'm sure your wings won't get in the way."

Another uproar of laughter. She turned apologetic eyes on Liam, who looked like he wanted to kill Sabine.

"Do you mind?" she asked softly. "I won't do it without your permission." When he shifted his gaze to her, she thought his expression held the slightest hint of excitement. The emotion was subtle though. Subtle enough she might be reading into it what she wanted to see.

"I don't mind." His answer was immediate although curt. His voice softened as he added, "Do your worst."

Slowly she took his face between her hands and

stared into his eyes. Rarely could Charlie feel the electricity in her blood that came with being celestial, but she could now. It was like Liam's gaze was a velvet hook, entering her and tugging at something low and deep within her. The intensity of the feeling made every other interaction she'd ever had with the opposite sex seem like a shadow of a true emotion. Her gaze dropped to his lips.

"It's okay with me, Charlotte," Liam said softly. "But you don't have to do this if you don't want to. I'll back you up if you refuse."

"I want to." Their eyes met and held. She leaned forward and pressed her mouth to his.

The kiss was friendly. Soft heat brushed her closed mouth. He kissed her the same way she might kiss her mother on the cheek. But it didn't stay that way. His large hand settled on the side of her head, and suddenly everything became far more complex. His lips danced with hers, fitting between her own with tiny nibbles and gentle suction. The roughness of his short beard was a delicious counter to his soft lips. And when his tongue grazed hers, lightning shot straight to her core.

By the time she realized where she was and drew away from him, her breath was coming in shaky pants. Slowly the world came back into focus and the cheers and whoops of the vampires filled her ears. Her cheeks turned hot and she looked away, breaking the connection between them. Liam's hand slipped slowly from her hair.

"I am satisfied," Elsa said.

The circle had made it around to Metluk, who stared down his nose at Liam like a master chastising an unruly dog. "Your turn. What do you choose, human?"

EIGHT

All the blood had rushed from Liam's head and straight to his dick. Damn, he couldn't remember wanting anyone like he wanted Charlotte at that moment. Definitely not Victoria or any of his previous girlfriends. He wrestled his libido back under his control and turned back to the game.

"What do you choose, human?" the one who'd burned his own hand asked. Well, he didn't plan to invite that type of thing.

"Ruse," he said.

Metluk drummed his fingers on his thigh, his gaze darting between Cassius, Charlotte, and him. Liam braced himself for something twisted. These vamps seemed to feed off humiliation and degradation.

"What event in your life are you the most ashamed of?"

Fucker. Liam narrowed his eyes on the asshole. Could he lie? After all, no one knew him here.

"Whatever you do, tell the truth," Charlotte whispered in his ear, her warm breath distracting him from the question. "They can smell a lie. Literally."

When she pulled away again, he rubbed his jaw and then rested his elbows on his knees. He knew the answer to this question, but he hated this story, and it was more personal than he'd have shared with Charlie if he'd had a choice. Still, if these vampires could in fact smell a lie, he'd rather tell the truth than face a risk challenge. He thought for a minute how to tell the story in a way this group would understand.

"The fire grows low," Cassius said with annoyance.

Liam cut a dagger-filled gaze in his direction, then began. "Some years ago, I was an Army Ranger assigned to a special operation in a war-torn area of my world."

"Is an Army Ranger a type of soldier?" Charlie asked.

He nodded. "Yes. An elite soldier."

She nodded for him to continue.

"Our mission was to destroy a warehouse that contained a chemical that we believed was being used to manufacture a deadly neurotoxin that would be used against our soldiers. I was the scientist on the team, specially trained in biochemistry. Everything was going as planned until we arrived at the warehouse. One of our regiment planted explosives around the outside of the facility while I broke into the building and made sure there was nothing in there that would kill us if it went up in flames. On my way out, I noticed two teenagers playing soccer in a nearby field, far enough away they wouldn't be harmed by the blast but close enough that they'd feel it. It struck me as odd. We were under the cover of darkness in the middle of the night. What were they doing up? But I thought of them as kids, so I didn't trust my gut and returned to my group without reporting them.

"My partner was supposed to detonate the explosives on my okay. But before he could press the plunger, a soccer ball hit him in the stomach. It exploded, killing him instantly. Another member of my squadron shot the assailant, and I was able make it to the detonator and complete our mission. But my buddy was dead." He glanced around the fire, finding Charlotte riveted by his story, or maybe she was put off by it. He stared at her as he wrapped it up. "My biggest regret is not trusting my instincts and taking those two teens out when I had the chance."

Charlotte's lids fluttered, an unreadable expression on her face. Great. There went any hope of getting closer to her. She probably thought he was a child killer. He inwardly groaned. Why had that bastard made him reveal his most sensitive memory?

"You're a warrior," Charlie said under her breath, her eyes wide.

He sliced his head to the right. "Not anymore. Now

I'm just a scientist. I prefer to fight my battles in a more peaceful way."

Cassius rose from his seat. "I don't believe it. You're no warrior."

Liam hadn't said a thing that wasn't true. He turned to Metluk, waiting for him to verify his story. The other vampire sipped from his goblet and crossed his legs at the ankle. "I smell no lie, Cassius. I am satisfied."

Take that, fucker. Liam raised his gaze to meet Cassius's. The vampire lunged too fast for him to see, but a sudden sharp pain in Liam's neck told him he'd been bitten. Instinctively, he cocked his arm and thrust the heel of his palm into the vampire's Adam's apple while at the same time sweeping his leg behind Cassius's. He had no doubt that vampires were faster and more agile than he was, and his chances of success with this move were low. But his blood must have distracted the creature because the move actually worked. Cassius fell backward into the fire.

He was up again in the blink of an eye. Liam lowered himself into a crouch, braced for an attack. But the vampire stopped abruptly only inches from him as if he'd slapped a glass wall. It took a second for Liam to register that there was a shield of light between them... and it was coming from Charlotte.

"It's time to go," she snapped.

"Charlie," Cassius said. "We were just messing

around. Boys will be boys. I promise if you return to the fire, I won't touch your human again."

"One round, Cassius. That's all I promised you. Now we really must be going. Send my love to Demidicus."

She waved one hand in a polite goodbye, but Liam noticed she didn't drop her shield until they reached the carriage. The sound of the vampires' distant laughter faded as she closed the door on Nochtbend.

"By the Mountain, Liam, are you okay?" Her voice sounded shaky.

"Yeah, I think so." He pressed his fingers into the wound on his neck.

"I'm so sorry. I should have never put you in that position," Charlie said.

None of this was her fault, but he nodded anyway. When someone apologized, it was a gift you accepted. "It must be hard being a princess. I imagine you felt... obligated."

"Yes." She sighed. "I was. Our political relations with Nochtbend have been uneasy in the past, and Cassius and I have a romantic history. If I refused his invitation, I was afraid it would give him a reason to make my refusal into something it wasn't."

"Probably the right decision."

"You're hurt." She moved to the seat beside him and brushed his hand away to press her own fingers to the bite. A glow ignited at the point of contact and filled the carriage.

"Can you heal me?"

She winced. "Not exactly. But I can close the wound."

"Ow!" He jerked away from her fingers when a sharp, burning pain traveled through his neck.

"There. Not bleeding anymore."

"Because you cauterized it!" He winced, his fingers hovering over the burn.

"I'll get you some salve from Maiara when we're back at the palace. She'll heal you right up."

"Maiara, that's Alexander's mate?" He was starting to put the family together.

"Yes. I can't believe you remembered that. I think he only mentioned it once."

He rubbed his sore neck. "A lot about this trip is permanently seared into my memory."

Silence spread through the carriage once more, and Liam leaned against the seat, suddenly exhausted. It had been one hell of a long day.

"Thank you for standing up for me back there, when Valcrun asked about my wings."

He couldn't see her face in the shadows, but her voice had held genuine gratitude.

"It's no one's fucking business what you do with your wings in bed. It was a rude question. That whole thing back there... that guy Cassius was trying to get under your skin. I don't know what happened between you two, but he's not a friend."

The seat crinkled as she shifted. "We were a couple

for a while. I'm the princess of Paragon. There's a certain expectation that I'll eventually marry, and I'm regularly courted by dignitaries from other kingdoms. Most of those meetings don't ever turn into relationships. Very few show actual interest once we've met in person."

"Why not?"

"Isn't it obvious?"

"Not to me."

"I'm an angel. The only one. A complete freak of nature."

"I think you're beautiful. Beyond beautiful. Stunning." He leaned forward until the moonlight from the window washed across his face. "Let me see you, Princess."

His breath left him in a rush when she obeyed, glowing in the small space. He reached out and twisted a strand of her platinum hair around his finger, their eyes locking. He was tempted to lean in for another kiss, but she looked away.

"There's another reason I don't date much, something no one ever talks about, but I suspect is the real reason I can't find a mate."

"What's that?" When she paused, he added, "You can tell me anything. I'm not even from this world, remember? I'm not going to judge you."

"There was a legend about me before I was born."

"A *legend.* What, like they sang songs about your

coming or something?" The wound on his neck started to itch, and he scratched it gently.

"Yes, actually. Before my parents, dragons were forbidden from mating with witches. It was well known by everyone in Ouros that if the two were ever to have a child, that child would be a monster. People believed it for centuries. The folklore in our kingdom made the citizens here terrified of me. They've since come to accept me, but there's still an underlying fear. I think Cassius, being a vampire, was attracted to that. I was a challenge to him—something to do on a dare. That's why... Well, once he'd gotten what he wanted, he lost interest."

"Cassius is an idiot. And you know what? I think he saw what he was missing tonight, because if there's one thing that's easy enough to spot in another man of any species, it's jealousy."

She smiled in the darkness. "You're very kind."

Liam wasn't the type of man to play games or to lie to get what he wanted. "I'm kind because I genuinely like you, Charlotte, and after that kiss we shared, I'm having trouble keeping my eyes off you."

Her breath came more quickly and she leaned back against the seat again, extinguishing her glow and falling into shadows.

The carriage came to a stop.

"We're here," she said.

He reached for the door to open it for her.

"You don't have to, Liam."

"I was closer to the door. It's the polite thing to do."

"No. I mean you don't have to keep your eyes off me."

Liam swallowed hard. Damn it all to hell, he was in trouble.

NINE

Charlie thought she saw a ghost of a smile soften Liam's features, but it was gone before she could be sure. He opened the door, and they stepped out onto the well-lit walkway leading to the palace. Liam's smile and the mood were gone. He stared down at her, his face impassive. What she wouldn't give to know what he was thinking.

"I should take you to see Maiara about that bite," she said, breaking the silence and leading the way toward the palace.

His head sliced to the side. "It's fine. Already healing."

"At least allow me to put some salve on it. I have some in my room," she said over her shoulder.

"Okay." His eyes slid to hers and she saw it again, the softness, the hint of a smile. Oh, it made her heart beat harder. She wondered what he'd look like if he laughed.

She led him down the hall through the palace to her chambers. Her personal area of the Obsidian Palace consisted of three large rooms connected by a common area with a kitchenette. Two of the rooms were bedrooms with sitting areas and balconies. The third room was her ritual room, which contained all manner of books, herbs, and crystals used in her magical pursuits. Tonight the halls outside her chambers were empty, which was good because she didn't want one of her uncles to press her again about where Liam was sleeping. She didn't want to think about her uncles at all as she led him through the door into the common area and then gestured for him to follow her into her bedroom and the adjoining bath.

Liam would only be here for a matter of days. As soon as he'd helped her prepare for the party, he'd want to go back to his own world and his own life. She understood that there could never be anything real or long-term between them, and that was okay. She had no expectations. But she was attracted to him, far more so than she'd ever been to Cassius. When she looked at Liam, she felt things a woman was supposed to feel for a man, things she'd rarely felt before and never as strongly. She wasn't sure exactly where she wanted this to go, only that she was enjoying the ride.

She dug in a drawer for the salve and turned back to him. "Hold still. This may sting."

He pulled away, backing toward the door. "Sting? What is it?"

"Just a salve. Herbs, oils, probably some healing waters."

His eyes narrowed. "If they were healing, why would they sting?"

With a light laugh, she sent him an incredulous look. "Liam, are you afraid of the salve?"

He frowned. "I never said that."

"You didn't have to say it. You're practically running from the room."

"I'm not afraid of the salve," he said testily.

"Then let me put this on you."

She screwed off the cap and dug a finger in, but when she reached for him, he took another step back and then another until he was all the way into her bedroom.

"No."

She laughed at the way he stared at the sweet-smelling salve like it was animal dung. "No?"

"How do you know it's safe for humans?"

"Because my mother and my aunt use it and they are human."

"I thought your mother was a witch."

"Well, yes. But she's also human. An immortal human but still a human."

The scowl on his face grew deeper. "No. It will heal on its own."

Her shoulders sank. "Vampire bites are filthy. It could become infected."

"I'll take my chances."

Charlie placed a hand on her hip and stormed toward him. He retreated until his thighs hit the back of the sofa, then halted. She didn't stop until her face was mere inches from his own.

"By the Mountain, you are worse than my nephews! Man up and allow me to treat your wound, you pigheaded thundercolt!"

He stared down at her, the corners of his mouth twitching until a smile broke through his dark features, one that reached all the way to his eyes. "Pigheaded thundercolt?"

Although her heart danced at the sight of the smile, she refused to be distracted by its magic. Quickly she slapped her fingers onto his neck, smearing the salve over the bite.

"Oww." He winced, smile fading.

She leaned closer and blew across the salve, cooling the sting. Whether it still hurt or not she wasn't sure, but he seemed suitably distracted. She caught him watching her intently out of the corner of his eye.

"Better?"

He raised a hand to hover over the wound. "Yeah."

"Good." Closing the cap on the salve, she tried to pick up at the point she lost the smile. "In Paragon, a thundercolt is a newborn mountain horse who is so young he's afraid of thunder. I assume you know what pigheaded means."

"Yeah, we use that one."

His lips were delectably close. She caught herself staring at them. The memory of the kiss they'd shared around the fire in Nochtbend made her stomach do a funny little flip and her heart thump like she'd flown for miles.

"I should cover that with a bandage so it doesn't get all over everything." She pulled away and strode back toward the bathroom.

He followed after her, a playful and somewhat predatory glint in his eye. She was sure now—Liam was looking at her like a man looks at a woman he wants, and the thought made her pulse sing. Looking at him through her lashes, she pressed a square of gauze over the wound and taped it into place, breathing deeply of the eucalyptus scent of the salve and the heady, masculine scent of man underneath.

Her hands were still on him when he asked gruffly, "Did you mean what you said before in the carriage?"

So close. His breath skated across her face. She met his gaze, enjoying the spark the hot look he gave her ignited within her. "About giving you permission to look at me? Yes, I meant it."

His face took on that grumpy, churlish expression it had before, and she wondered if she'd made him angry. "I don't like to play games, Charlotte. You're beautiful. Mind-bendingly beautiful. But I'm not from here, and you know I can't stay. If I... look at you like I want to look at you... I... I don't want you to regret anything later. And I fucking never want it to get back to your uncles if you change your mind about anything that happens between us."

The straightforward way he talked about it was refreshing to her, although a bit sad. On the one hand, she knew exactly where he stood. He wanted her, the same as she wanted him. But it was sad how transactional it all sounded, the end of their relationship decided before they'd even begun. She turned away and started washing her hands so he wouldn't see the ridiculous and illogical disappointment on her face. "I know perfectly well the reality of our situation. If I give you permission, I give you permission. It's no one else's business but our own."

She dried her hands off and turned back to him, tension building between them until the air seemed to crackle. But as moments passed and all he did was look at her, her spirits fell. She wondered what it was: her wings, her general eagerness, her admittance that there wasn't much interest in her in Paragon. Why wouldn't he touch her? Kiss her again like before? All he did was stare, like she was a puzzle he was trying to solve. Eventually it made her uneasy and she had to act.

With a deep sigh, she stepped around him. "It's late. Let me show you to your room."

"'Kay," he murmured, striding after her as she crossed the common area to her guest room door. She threw it open and stepped inside. "There are extra blankets and towels in the wardrobe. Everything else you might need should be in the cabinet in the bathroom."

He stepped into the room behind her and closed the door, leaning his back against it.

She turned to him. "What are you doing?"

"You gave me permission to look at you. Can I touch you as well?"

She tilted her head. "Yes. Is that why you haven't—?"

"We've only known each other a day, Charlotte. I was trying to follow your lead." He pushed off the door and prowled toward her. "You're very hard to read."

"I'm not the one with a permanent scowl on my face." She laughed lightly.

His eyes turned dark and brooding. "Do not. You simply don't know me well enough to read my moods."

She raised an eyebrow. "No? Okay, show me what you're feeling right now."

He swallowed, his eyes taking on the hooded quality of a man possessed with desire. Heat flared deep in her torso.

"Am I scowling now?"

"No."

He stepped in closer, his hands taking her waist. His tongue licked along his bottom lip. "Can you guess what this expression is, Charlotte?"

She licked her own lips, suddenly breathless at his touch. "Hunger."

Another smile, this one darker, wolfish. "I think we started something beside that fire tonight that needs to be finished."

One large hand lifted, his fingers sliding into her hair, tugging at her scalp until she tipped her head back and gasped. The sound seemed to ignite something within him. His mouth met hers, capturing that tiny gasp, swallowing it whole. She melted against him.

He wasn't gentle as their mouths collided, and she liked that. She was immortal, powerful enough to hurt him if she wanted to. He'd witnessed some of that tonight. And maybe that was why he gripped her tightly against him, almost desperately. She nipped his bottom lip and he growled, repositioning his mouth. His tongue swept in, tangling with hers, kindling something deep within her with every stroke.

She leaned more heavily against him. He spun her around until her back and wings were against the wall. Moving her feet farther apart, she pulled him closer so he could settle between her slightly bent knees. His body stretched against hers, his erection pressed long and hard against the sensitive spot between her legs. Rolling her hips, she rubbed against him. Mountain help her, he felt big everywhere. She wondered what a human looked like down there, if his dick was as big and broad as it felt. What that would feel like inside her. In her hand? In her mouth? Pounding into her?

He groaned, grinding against her. Both hands gripped her waist, then skimmed up her sides, his thumbs flicking across the tips of her breasts under her tunic. A soft moan left her throat, and he kissed her again. His hands kept going, sliding up her back to the base of her wings. She sighed at the feeling. His fingers in her feathers made her rub herself against him more urgently.

"My god, Charlotte, what are you doing to me?" he whispered against her lips. "I can't stop touching you." Gently he stroked the edges of her feathers, tracing her outer wing before he returned to massaging the place where they met her back.

"That feels incredible," she whispered against his mouth.

He kept going for a bit before wrapping his hand around the back of her neck and drawing back to look at her.

She reached between their bodies for his fly, popping his top button to work her hand inside his pants. But he caught her wrist, a strange, almost pained look crossing his face. "Wait."

"Why, what's wrong?" His eyes focused on her

wings and her blood ran cold to think he might reject her because of what she was.

"There really isn't anyone like you, is there?"

"Not on this world or your own." She couldn't keep her voice from sounding clipped. "Does that bother you?"

He shook his head. "No," he said breathlessly. "It's just a reminder that you're special. I can't treat you like any other woman, Charlotte."

"Because I'm *different*." The last word was laden with disgust as she pulled her hand from his waistband.

He chewed his lip. Running his hand down her arm, he tangled his fingers into hers before grinding himself against her once more. "Yes, you are, but that's just the thing, Princess—you are a rare and glorious gift, and I want to savor you. And I can't do that when I feel like I might fall asleep on my feet at any moment."

All at once, she noticed the bags under his eyes and the way he was using the wall for support. "Oh."

"I'm only human."

Of course he was, and she'd dragged him across dimensions and then over half of Ouros. He'd lost blood too, from the bite. "You should lie down."

He leaned against her one more time, his nostrils flaring as if he were drawing in her scent. His voice was raspy as he added, "This type of thing, it's always better when you get to know someone first. Get to know what they like... what they need."

She wasn't sure exactly what he meant by that. Her times with Cassius had been quick and left her wanting more. But she took Liam's hand and led him to the bed. She pulled back the covers, and he crawled in with a groan as his body melted into the mattress.

She'd begun to move for the door when his voice rang out. "Stay."

"Hmm?"

"Stay with me, Charlotte." He blinked at her from his pillow.

She toed off her boots and climbed in beside him. In truth, she wasn't tired. She could go days without sleeping. But she liked being with him, and part of her wanted to watch him sleep. She caught him staring at her wings again.

"I can use magic to temporarily store my wings inside myself if you want me to," she offered.

He grunted, his big hand landing heavily on her waist. "Why would you do that?"

"They take up a lot of space in bed. Don't be surprised if you get a face full of feathers." Cheeks hot, she looked at him again. "I mean, I can stop that from happening if it's too weird for you."

With a gritty laugh, he yanked her against him, his lips brushing hers. "It's not weird for me. I like it. Is it more comfortable for you?"

"No. It feels... crowded. I only do it when I have to."

"Then keep them right where they are." He closed his eyes, his head sinking deeper into the pillow.

Charlotte watched all the tension drain from his face and shoulders as his breath evened out and he drifted easily to sleep.

Liam woke to the scent of sunlight, citrus, and new grass and a face full of feathers. He smiled as he opened his eyes, a warm, peaceful feeling coming over him. For a split second, he'd wondered if she'd been a dream, but he was not imagining the heat from her body or the light from Paragon's two suns streaming from the balcony.

Bracing his head on his hand, he gazed down at her. Fuck, she was beautiful. His dick twitched just thinking about that kiss last night. And it didn't bother him at all that she wasn't human. Maybe that was the most surprising thing. But in a way, she made more sense to him. She was her own thing, her own person, her own species. Every woman he'd met before her seemed ordinary and mundane in comparison. He desperately wanted to know her better, to discover everything about her.

Brow furrowing, his thoughts caught up to his libido. He had to be careful. What he was describing bordered on real feelings—thinking she was special, wanting to get to know her better. He shook his head. He couldn't get attached. This was a temporary arrangement. He was an explorer on a voyage in outer space. Eventually he'd have to go back to Earth.

But that didn't mean he couldn't explore her while he was here. He moved closer to her, nestling between her wings and working his hand under one to splay across her belly.

"Mmm. Good morning," she said over her shoulder.

"Morning." He brushed his lips over her ear as he worked his hand under her shirt, stroking along her belly, up to cup her breast and tease her nipple.

She rewarded him by grinding her ass against his cock.

He took that as an invitation to keep going. With long, languid strokes, he smoothed down her torso, teasing under her waistband, then up again to knead each of her breasts and pluck at her nipples. He loved the way it made her squirm.

After several long and languid strokes, he paused, hand splayed against her skin. "You don't have a belly button."

She shook her head and smiled at him over her shoulder. "Dragons hatch from eggs. So did I."

He went perfectly still behind her. But when her

face turned somber, he realized that his reaction was causing her pain. This was a woman who'd admitted being rejected again and again. And he was man enough not to add to whatever insecurities were plaguing her.

He rolled her onto her back and shifted on top of her. The wings weren't a problem at all, tucked under her as if she were wearing a feathered cape. He pulled up her shirt and took a good look at her navelless belly. "Beautiful."

"Really?" Her blue eyes twinkled up at him.

In response, he shifted down her body and licked over the spot a human navel would reside.

"Oh."

Fuck, she tasted good. That sunshine-and-citrus scent of hers translated to a sweetness that clung to her skin. He had to know more. He reached for the waistband of her pants.

"This okay?" he asked, looking up at her through his lashes. Her scent, the sunlight and warmth of this room—he almost felt drunk on it, but he wouldn't do anything without her consent.

"You're not tired anymore?" Her cheeks warmed with color.

He shook his head.

"Then it's okay."

He pulled her pants down over her hips and then off her legs, casting them aside. "Let me see you." Gently he pressed against her inner thighs, spreading her wider. The sound that came from his chest was one he didn't know he was capable of making. Did he just growl?

"Is there something wrong with me?" His gaze drifted to her face to find it lined with worry. Here he was with a raging hard-on, obsessing over her, and she thought he was weirded out by it.

"Fuck no. You're beautiful."

Her smile made that warm feeling in his chest uncoil again, Shifting between her knees, he ran his hands up her thighs until his thumbs brushed her core. Lightly, he stroked her center and circled her clit. That, to his relief, seemed identical to human anatomy, which meant they were going to have one hell of a good time.

"But...Is my body strange to you?" Her voice was soft, tentative. She really didn't know how beautiful she was, and wasn't that a refreshing surprise?

He had to clear his throat to find his voice. It was all gravel as he responded. "Hell no, Princess. You're fucking perfect. Absolutely perfect."

Her face lit up with a crazy smile, and damn if that didn't send liquid fire through his veins. He rewarded her by circling his thumb over her again, then running his knuckle up her slit.

She tipped her head back and closed her eyes. "Mmm."

"Watch me, Princess," he commanded, rubbing her in circles while he studied her reaction.

She obeyed, and fuck it turned him on. Her breath came in parts as she stared at him working her sex, and soon her hips got in on the action, trying to chase the pleasure he longed to give her.

"You're so wet. I think you're ready for more." He slid a finger inside her, her tight, wet heat making his dick pulse in anticipation. "Fuck, Charlotte..."

She moved faster, riding his hand harder. He added another finger, rubbing circles deep within her while his thumb continued working her clit. She was writhing now, fisting the sheets.

"Come for me, angel. Come for me."

Charlotte cried out, her body arching off the mattress as her skin lit up like a rising sun. "Fuuuuck!"

That was unexpected. Light and heat washed over him until it almost burned. Her pleasure shone through her skin, her body becoming an exploding star. The light was almost blinding. A small part of him wondered if he should be afraid, but he cast the thought aside. His life wasn't that precious to him. He was more than willing to be consumed by her, by this.

But as she sank back down on the mattress, he wasn't harmed in any way by the energy he'd drawn out of her. She came together again and stared up at him in blatant wonder, her lids low, her lips parted.

"Mountain, Liam. I've never felt anything like that."

It took him a second to realize what she was

saying. But that couldn't be right. "Wait, do you mean you've never had an orgasm?"

She shook her head.

"Princess Charlie?" A distant voice came through the door.

Her eyes widened and she leaped out from under him, a look of panic on her face.

"It's my lady's maid!" She swiped her pants off the end of the bed and pulled them on. "Stay here."

He nodded. Where else would he go?

Smoothing her hair, she slipped from the room, leaving him feeling cold and empty in her absence. Fuck, he was in trouble, and not just because he had a major case of blue balls.

AN HOUR LATER LIAM FOUND HIMSELF IN THE PALACE kitchen, running his fingers through a substance Charlotte called flour. It was white. It was powdery. But the texture reminded him more of almond flour than wheat flour, and the scientist in him was attempting to divine its chemical composition from touch and smell alone.

"What is this made from?" he asked her.

"Barrel root, from the volcanic side of the mountain."

He nodded. "Only one way to find out if it's the same as flour from Earth."

He grabbed a large bowl from the rack and measured in a couple of cups. He'd decided to make chocolate chip cookies. They weren't exactly Christmas related, but it was the only recipe he had memorized. Thankfully, Paragon's salt and sugar were identical to what he was used to. Baking soda and vanilla extract he'd have to improvise.

"Is there anything I can do to help?" she asked as he perused the contents of the pantry.

He glanced back at her, that damned warm feeling blooming in his chest again. "Talk to me. Tell me about yourself." It occurred to him that he should be asking about the composition of the soil or where Paragon was in the universe—scientific questions—but all his dumbass brain wanted to know was more about her. What made her tick? What was it like for her growing up in this place? Maybe her favorite flower and how she liked her coffee.

She seemed surprised at the request, her wings rising. "What do you want to know?"

"Start with this legend you were telling me about yesterday. Why would anyone think you'd be a monster?"

Charlotte leaned against one of the steel counters and started to talk, and the story she told rivaled any novel he'd ever read. Thousands of years ago an empress named Eleanor had murdered her own brother and his witch mate, who was one of three powerful sisters. Their unborn child, who would have been like Charlotte, was killed with his mother. Publicly, Eleanor spun it as self-defense and they outlawed all mating between dragons and witches because it fit their narrative. For hundreds of years, the people of Ouros had told stories and sung songs about the monster child of a witch and a dragon. So when Charlotte's witch mother mated her dragon father, there was naturally trepidation.

Only, over time, her father was able to reveal Eleanor's true colors and take back the kingdom from his wicked, murderous mother. Charlotte's birth fulfilled the prophecy of the three sisters, but not in the way everyone assumed. By overthrowing Eleanor, her family brought peace to the kingdom.

She told him about her journey into the underworld with her uncle Marius—another uncle!—and how she'd spent her childhood learning to control her celestial powers while expanding her practice of witch magic, a skill she learned from her mother, along with traditional dragon magic she learned in school.

"So you went to school." He stopped stirring the concoction in front of him to concentrate on her. "No private tutors for the princess?"

She smiled. "I think my father would have preferred private tutors, but my mother wanted me to have as normal a childhood as possible. I attended Rawkfist Academy. It's a private school here in Paragon. My parents were worried at first because I'm different, but I wasn't bullied much, surprisingly. I think they were too afraid of me to bully me. My biggest obstacle was getting people to see beyond my royal title and the disparaging folklore to interact with me at all. A few did. My best girlfriends are people I met there."

"Did you go to university?" he asked, pulling a pan from the rack and heaping balls of dough onto it. It smelled like chocolate chip cookie dough, but the texture wasn't quite right.

She glanced at him. "Yes. As far as I could go. My specialty is metaphysics and sorcery."

He chuckled.

"What's so funny?"

"That wouldn't even be a real major in my world."

"Oh?" She snorted. "What did you study?"

"I have a PhD in environmental sciences, which means I took an unholy amount of chemistry, physics, and biology as well as earth science."

"Sounds terribly boring." She laughed.

"Never!" he admonished. "I bet you didn't know that an entire ecosystem lives in a drop of our ocean water. Millions of microscopic organisms populate the surface along with an unfortunate amount of microscopic plastic and chemicals. That's my passion, reducing the concentration of harmful stuff in our oceans."

Charlie narrowed her eyes. "If it's harmful, why is it there?"

He sighed. "Humans don't have magic, so sometimes we have to use plastic."

She giggled. "Plastic is like magic?"

Sliding the pans into the strange round oven, he sighed. "As much as I hate to admit it, it's superlight and has a million applications, many of them lifesaving. It's not a simple problem. I'm not sure the human race could ever completely go back to living without it."

"If there is a way to save your Earth from this complex problem, I know that you will figure it out. You're very smart."

He chuckled. "What makes you think so?"

"How you handled Cassius when he attacked you. Many people would have panicked in that situation."

He sighed. "That was training, not intelligence."

"From your days as a warrior."

"Yeah. The Army."

"So you left your family business, joined your military, educated yourself, and now you're working to save your planet? And your family has pushed you away?"

"That's about right."

"Hmm. I'm sorry about that. My family is everything to me. I wish yours treated you better. You deserve better."

His heart squeezed at her words and the way she looked at him, as if she found him worthy. Valuable. As much as he was tempted to let the conversation go at that, Liam wanted to tell her the truth. If there was anyone he could tell, it was her. In a few days, he'd never see her again, and because she was from another world, there was no one she could tell.

"The truth is, it's not entirely their fault." He clenched his jaw.

"Oh?" She leaned forward slightly. No judgment, just interest.

"My dad and I didn't get along when I was a kid, and I couldn't wait to get out of the house. Yes, we had our differences, but I was the one who left. They never kicked me out. And the door has always remained open for me to come home. Don't get me wrong, they aren't kind people. I'm not missing any warm family memories. But they also aren't the ones who ended our relationship. That was me. He died in August, and I know my mom probably needed me, but I stayed away."

She tilted her head. "I don't understand. Were they accepting of your choices or not?"

He sighed. "At first my father was angry, but he didn't need me in the business. He had my brother Spencer and sister Kara to carry the weight. Over time, he dropped it. But I felt the disdain every time I came home. My parents would spew praises about my siblings. When it came to me and my life, they never said a word... until I became engaged to a socialite."

"You're engaged?"

"*Was* engaged. It's over. My family thought she'd

force me to settle down and get with their program for my life. It's what she wanted. But that life wasn't for me."

"You don't want to settle down."

"I don't want to work for Morrismart. I wouldn't mind having a family someday, but not with her. Not when it's all about the money and the name."

She frowned. "I can relate to that." Hanging her head, she traced the toe of her slipper across the wood floor. "I can't tell you how many men have come here, hoping to become a prince, only to see my wings and decide the title wasn't worth it."

He shook his head. "They have no idea what they're missing, angel. Your wings…" He fixed her with a hungry look. "I think I like waking up with feathers in my face."

She raised an eyebrow.

He stroked the length of one wing. "I think you may have ruined me for wingless women."

Their eyes locked and held, her cheeks turning a delicious shade of pink. She spun away to check the cookies, breaking the tension and snapping him out of the moment. This was a dangerous game they were playing.

"You were saying, about your family…?"

Liam shifted. He was getting painfully close to sharing more about himself than he should. Charlotte was not a potential girlfriend. She wasn't even human. She was, for all intents and purposes, an alien, and their relationship would last only long enough for him to serve his purpose to her and return home. He was here to learn and nothing more.

"Charlotte, there's something we should discuss. What happened this morning between us can never happen again."

The smile faded from her face. "I'm sorry we were interrupted. I can have a talk with my maid—"

"No, that's not it. There can't be anything between us. This situation is temporary and... getting closer to each other, it can only complicate things."

"But... what about what you just said...? I thought you liked the wings—"

"I do." He raked his gaze down her body. "I like all of you, Princess, and if we'd met under different circumstances, I bet we'd have a go at trying our best to become sick of each other. After what I saw this morning, I wouldn't let you out of bed for a week."

"Then why?" Deep disappointment lined her mouth.

He shrugged. "It's obvious. We're from different worlds. This can't last. And I realized just now, talking to you, that as powerful as you are, you're also sweet and inexperienced. The last thing you need in your life is a man like me. I'd be using you. I can't give you more than that, and it's far less than you deserve."

For a moment she seemed to consider that. "After this morning, I wonder if I might be using you."

"If I believed for a moment that were the case, I'd

have no problem being used." He frowned. That asshole Cassius had treated her like she was disposable. Damn if he'd repeat that experience for her. She deserved so much better.

"Fine." She straightened. "Then it won't happen again."

"Good."

"Now. You were saying about your family... What made you miss your father's funeral? It sounds like although you had your differences, your family still cares for you."

"I don't want to talk about it."

She flinched. "Something else happened. Something beyond your disagreement about the business."

He rolled his lips. "Yeah. I will say that part of me regrets it. A small part. I recognize that maybe I should have been there for my mother despite everything. But what's done is done."

"It doesn't have to be." She studied him.

"Yes it does. It's safer. Bridging the distance between us would be a monumental undertaking at this point. Believe me when I say it would be easier on everyone if I avoid it."

"Easier isn't always better, Liam. Sometimes life is complicated and painful, but I'd rather have that than live a life where I felt nothing." She looked down at her fingers. "A life without passion is just a pretty cage."

He wasn't sure now if she was still talking about his family or what happened between them. Not worth diving into. The best thing he could do right now was to set clear boundaries with her. He'd already shared too much, felt feelings he didn't want to feel, and he'd barely known her a day.

She stepped closer to him, the heat from her body making his fingers twitch to touch her.

"Do you want to know what I think?" Her voice was low, seductive. "I think that you've let this gap between you and your family go on for so long and grow so wide that it's not confronting them that you fear anymore but learning that the separation is too much to undo. You fear contempt. You're afraid they just won't care anymore. And part of you wants that, just like you want it with me. Instead of having an experience with me, one that will end, sure, but might be... memorable, you want the separation. You want to be numb. Because as much as you fear contempt, as much as you fear that there is nothing, you fear feeling something far more."

Boom. The crushing weight of the truth made his chest ache. Was this part of her powers? Could she see into his soul? There was a part of him that understood his mother was as much a victim of his father as he was. And the longer they went without speaking, the more he wondered, somewhere in his subconscious, if she still cared, if she still thought of him as her son. Her request that he come to Christmas this year indicated that she did. He wasn't sure why it mattered to him, only knew that it did. And Charlotte was right about his feelings about her as well. He didn't want to play too close to this flame. It felt too good licking up his body.

"Feelings just complicate things." He shook his head.

"Yeah, they do." The heart-stopping smile she gave him almost distracted him from the smell wafting through the kitchen. Grateful for the distraction, he grabbed a towel and used it to pull the pan out, tossing it on top of the oven.

"I think they're done," he said. He wasn't sure. The cookies were perfectly round, golden brown, and smooth as glass. He frowned. Those were like no chocolate chip cookies he'd ever seen in his life.

Her hand shot out and grabbed one, lifting it toward her mouth.

"Wait, they're hot!"

"I'm impervious to heat. I can walk through fire and it won't burn me."

She brought the cookie toward her lips. Snatching her wrist, he stopped her from taking a bite. "I'm not sure you should eat that."

"Why not?"

"It's not normal. I think something went wrong."

She sighed. "It's going to be different here. We have different ingredients."

"But what if it's not good? I should try it first."

The laugh she answered with made her face light

up. "Liam, are you attempting to protect me from this cookie? How noble of you."

"I'm not noble, I just—"

"As sweet as that is, I think I can handle it." She tugged her arm away with surprising strength and took a bite. He watched as she chewed, her face unreadable. After a few chews, she held the bit cookie out to him. "You have to try this!"

And wasn't that just erotic as hell. He wasn't sure why, but her feeding him was the hottest thing he could remember happening to him in a long, long time. He met her eyes before leaning in and biting over her bite.

Her enchanting gaze distracted him, and it took a second to realize something was off. The cookie tasted sweet but crumbled in his mouth like dirt. No, not dirt, it was like having a mouthful of Grape-Nuts. He chewed and chewed, grimacing at the awful texture. "This is—"

"Awful?" she added, laughing and pitching the remains of the cookie on the tray. "Not fit for dragon consumption?"

"You knew and you made me try it anyway?"

She laughed harder. "I needed someone else to share the horror of the experience."

He squinted at her and spit the remains of the cookie into a rubbish bin. A wicked grin split his face. "You are a bad angel."

She shrugged. "Are you going to punish me for my

crimes? Anything but making me eat another Christmas cookie."

"Oh, I have other ideas," he said darkly.

He reached for her, but she sprinted from his grasp, giggling. He chased after her, out of the kitchen and down the hall, laughing in a way that he hadn't since, when, third grade maybe? *Fuck*, he wasn't sure what he'd do when he caught her, but it wouldn't involve pain. Despite his earlier promise to keep his hands off her, the only thing he wanted to give her was pleasure.

He closed in, reaching for her waist as she squealed over her shoulder. And that's when a large hand shot out from the shadows and clotheslined him.

ELEVEN

"Uncle Colin, stop!" Charlotte raced to Liam's side, relieved when she saw he was still breathing, albeit more of a wheeze. The hollow sound of his head hitting the obsidian floor had been cringe-worthy, and he'd clearly had the breath knocked out of him. Praise the Mountain, there was no blood, but Colin's hand around his throat did not appear gentle.

"Who the hell is this, Charlie?" Colin released Liam's throat but fisted the hand, flexing his scarred arm as if he wasn't afraid to use it if he needed to.

"He's my friend," Charlotte said, pushing her uncle's hands away and checking Liam's head and neck for injuries. "Call Maiara," she commanded a servant at the end of the hall. "I think he's hurt."

"He's not hurt," Colin grumbled. "He's just catching his breath."

"He's human, Uncle. Not a dragon. You could have cracked his skull."

Colin grimaced. "Human? What the fuck is a human doing chasing you down the hall?"

She glared at him. "He's my guest."

Colin's jaw clenched. "Your guest?"

"I brought him here. He's helping me with a special project."

"A human? Where did you even find a human?"

"Earth."

Colin stiffened. "Do your parents know you left Paragon?"

She was saved from answering when Maiara arrived with her bag and started assessing Liam.

"Fine," Liam mumbled, but his eyes rolled back in his head. He was most certainly not fine.

"You will be," Maiara said, placing her healing amulet around his neck.

The caregiving did not distract Uncle Colin from their conversation. He was like a dragon with a bone. "Charlie..."

She glared at him. "Nothing happened. I was only there for a moment."

"It's a risk."

"A risk I was willing to take." She turned back to Liam, but Colin grabbed her arm.

"Charlie... you're smarter than that."

She tugged her arm away from him. "It's a theory,

nothing more. For all we know, it's a completely unnecessary level of caution."

Liam sat up, holding his head, and Maiara removed her amulet from his chest. She held up one finger. "Rest, one hour. No more fighting."

Liam nodded and Maiara took off in the direction of the infirmary. His eyes darted between Colin and her. "I'm Liam. You look like... that is to say, you must be..."

Colin snorted, smiling despite the tightness in his jaw. "I am Colin, master of the Obsidian Guard and, yes, Sylas's twin and Charlie's uncle. Sorry for the confusion. I didn't realize you were Charlie's guest."

"Uh, yeah, honest mistake." His eyes shifted away as he waved two fingers dismissively.

Charlie hooked her arm under Liam's. "Come on, I'll help you back to my room."

"Your room? He's staying in your room?" A muscle in Uncle Colin's jaw jumped with his demand for answers. .

"I'm fine, really," Liam said to her.

"Maiara will have both our heads if we don't follow her orders."

"Why is he staying in your room?" A growl rumbled in Colin's chest.

Charlie turned to face him head-on. "Uncle Colin, what exactly brings you to this wing of the palace?"

"Leena sent me. She wanted me to tell you that the

tree you had delivered from Everfield is in the great hall. She would have come herself, but she's transcribing some notes for the queen."

Charlie turned to Liam excitedly. "It's here! Okay, you still have to rest, but then we'll see the tree." She tugged his hand toward her chambers.

"Charlie, about what I said before...," Colin called.

"I've got it under control, Uncle." She hurried down the hall and was relieved when he didn't follow. A few minutes later, she had Liam tucked into her second bedroom.

"What was your uncle talking about? He said you put yourself at risk." Liam blinked up at her from his pillow, looking exhausted.

"He thought you were an attacker because you were chasing me," Charlie said dismissively. There was far more to it than that, but she didn't need another man on her case about it.

"No, not that part. The part where he implied it was dangerous for you to leave Paragon?"

"Just being overprotective. I'll wake you in an hour." She pulled the door closed between them.

After a rest that ended up lasting two hours, Charlie led Liam to the great hall and beamed when she saw the tree. The massive pot it was in anchored the magnificent specimen, which rose almost to the rafters at the center of the round room.

Liam walked up to it, his mouth falling open. "When you said they wouldn't kill it, I assumed they were going to cut off the top or something. How did they manage potting it? This tree is massive."

"Probably sang to it," Charlie said.

When Liam turned disbelieving eyes on her, she shrugged. "Fairies have a special relationship with trees. When they build their homes, they sing to the trees to coax them into the shapes they want."

"Incredible." He slid his fingers over one of the branches. "But how does it work? Are the trees here... sentient? Or are their singing voices acting on the plants at the cellular level?"

"Neither. It's magic. Fairy magic." Charlie loved how fascinated he was by something she took for granted.

"But how does the magic work?" Liam's expression was nothing short of puzzled.

She moved in closer to him, trailing her fingers along the edge of the pot. "It's in their blood, their celestial energy, the vibration of their souls, the ancestral roots of their species. Their voices hold the power of generations."

He shook his head, laughing. "That makes no sense."

"How hard did you hit your head?" She smirked at him.

"You know what I mean. You're an educated woman. There has to be an explanation for how things work. Things don't just happen. Trees don't uproot themselves for a song." His jaw clenched, and Charlie was worried he might come out of his skin.

"Liam, do women have wings where you come from?"

He met her gaze. "Uh, no."

"But I do, and I'm standing right in front of you. How do my wings work? Why was I born with them?"

"We could find out with an MRI, some blood tests. There's an explanation. There always is." He frowned.

She tucked her hair behind her ears. "And how did I get you here from your world? Is there an explanation for that?"

"Must be."

"You're right, there is. Magic. Ancient magic."

"I don't believe in magic." He cast her one of his trademark scowls.

Her brows shot up to her hairline fast enough that she felt her ears lift. "What a dark existence you must have if you can only believe in the things you fully understand."

"I don't have to fully understand them to know that there is a scientific explanation. There's an order to things. What appears to be magic has a rational cause and effect, possibly something that hasn't been discovered yet but still it exists."

"Challenge accepted." She extended her hand to him. "Come with me."

"Where are we going?"

"To my ritual room. I am going to demonstrate some magic for you, and in the process, we are going to decorate this tree, a tree that crawled out of the ground and into this pot using magic."

"You won't change my mind."

She narrowed her eyes. "We'll see about that."

LIAM TOOK HER HAND, ALLOWING HER TO LEAD HIM BACK TO her chambers. He still had a throbbing headache, and he wasn't sure if it was from his head hitting the floor or the unbelievable sight of the potted tree in the great hall. He supposed it would be possible to move a tree like that with heavy machinery, maybe an excavator and a crane, but how did they get it into the hall so quickly?

Ah, he was being dim. Considering they were on a different planet, the machinery here must be more advanced. All this nonsense about magic was simply Charlotte's way of making sense of the world she was in, but with the right equipment, he could puzzle out the physics of it. For now he'd simply accept that it was possible with the technology these creatures possessed.

Charlotte led him through a door off the central

area of her apartment and into a room that belonged on a movie set. A large symbol was painted on the floor, surrounded by shelves of candles, herbs, crystals and bones. It was like he'd been transported into one of those touristy magic shops in the city that preyed on people's psychological problems in order to sell them bags of polished rocks.

"You said before that Christmas trees usually have lights, right?" She handed him a pad of paper. "What do they look like?"

Liam was no artist, but he did his best to sketch a tree with Christmas lights.

"That's lovely."

He had to swallow down a sudden swell of emotion when visions of his childhood tree danced in his head. He'd unwittingly drawn one to look the same. "I grew up in an egregiously large estate in upstate New York, and my parents used to have a professional come in and put up our Christmas decorations. All white lights and perfectly spaced ornaments." He scoffed and rolled his eyes. "The place was like a department store window. But they used to let Spencer, Kara, and me decorate the tree in our basement because no one went down there but us. It looked just like that with gaudy, multicolored lights and homemade ornaments. I loved it."

With a wink, she said, "Then this is the tree we will have." She carried the sketch back to her workbench and reached for a coil of gold wire. "What colors were those lights?"

When she held out a box to him, he padded to her side. It was filled with gemstones of all shapes, sizes, and colors. He picked up a large sapphire and held it up to the light. It couldn't be real, but damn if it wasn't a perfect replica.

Charlotte took the stone from his hand and wrapped it securely in the wire. "More. What other colors?"

The stones were a far cry from Christmas lights, but hey, maybe like the cookies, this was the best they could do here. He tossed her jewels one after the other in the order of the multi-colored lights he remembered as a kid. Soon, Charlotte had crafted a long string of gems that at least reflected the light in a way that was breathtaking.

"This is similar to your Christmas lights?"

"Close enough. In my world, they're electric lights like the kind that light this room." He pointed to her desk lamp.

Charlotte glanced at the light with an impish smile. "Electric, huh?"

He nodded.

She coiled the strand of gems loosely around her fist and stepped into the symbol at the center of the room, placing them near her feet. "All the lights in Paragon use energy from the volcano—geothermal energy—that's transformed into light using magic. Magic similar to this." She raised her hands on either side of her body and started to chant. What she said made no sense to him. It might have been Latin or Greek, but he didn't recognize a word of it. The effects were something he'd never forget. Her eyes glowed pure white, and an electrical storm crackled between her hands, larger and more violent until it struck the coiled gems with a thunderous boom that had him backing up a step. Charlotte lowered her hands and lifted the gems off the smoking floor.

What the fuck? Liam stepped toward her. The gems were now lit from within and bright enough to cast colorful light around the room. Mouth gaping, he reached out to touch one.

"Oww!" He snatched his hand back, blowing on his fingers.

"Careful," she said. "They'll cool off eventually, but it will take time."

"But you're touching them."

She laughed. "I told you before. I'm fireproof like my father. I'll put them here until they're safe for you." She placed the strand into a deep metal cauldron. "Why don't we start on the ornaments while we're waiting?"

"But... But... How long will they stay lit like that?"

She shrugged. "As long as I'm alive."

He shook his head. "How?"

Rolling her eyes, she closed the space between

them and took his face in her hands. "Magic, Liam. It's magic."

He stared at the lights winding round and round inside the belly of that metal pot, and all he could think was that he'd fallen down the rabbit hole and he wasn't sure he'd ever find his way out. Scarier still, he wasn't sure he wanted to. Maybe he'd hit his head harder than he thought.

TWELVE

Later that evening, Charlotte finished putting the lights on the massive tree in the great hall and started decorating it with glass spheres she'd had a servant purchase from an artisan in Hobble Glen. Liam said they were a good likeness to the ones he was familiar with. After he'd helped her for some time, she could tell he needed rest and had Cook bring him dinner. At the moment, he was scarfing down a narwit burger with blue chips and enjoying his third glass of tribiscal wine.

"This wine is delicious." He held the glass up to the light. "If I could re-create this on Earth, I'd make a mint."

"You might have trouble with that. Tribiscal fruit trees only grow in volcanic soil, and the fruit has to be harvested by hand."

"We have volcanic soil. I'll start a vineyard on the big island of Hawaii."

"I've never even heard of that place." She sighed, her smile turning wistful.

"No?"

"I haven't spent time on Earth since I was a child."

He took another gulp of his wine before asking, "Why not?"

"Just never had a reason, I guess."

He leaned back in his chair, crossing his legs at the ankle. "Bullshit. You said you have an aunt who owns an art gallery in New York and an uncle who's married to a vampire in Chicago. Also, your entire reason for throwing this Christmas, despite it clearly not being Christmas here, was to impress your mother and aunt who are from Earth. That sounds like at least four reasons to visit, yet you haven't."

She busied herself placing another ornament, then dusted off her hands. "I think the tree is looking good."

"I think you're avoiding telling me the truth about why your uncle Colin was worried about you leaving Paragon and why you haven't spent more time on Earth even though you have connections there."

She whirled on him. "Don't act like I'm the only one with secrets. It's pretty clear to me that there's a reason you don't believe in magic or relationships. Something more than just a tiff with your family over the environmental friendliness of their business. There was a reason you didn't go to your father's funeral and a reason you were hiding at the North Pole during the human holidays."

He worked his jaw back and forth before draining the last of his wine. "Fine, we both have secrets."

She turned and stared up at the tree. "It's late and we need to finish decorating this tree. What's this thing you've drawn on top?"

"A star. It's usually made out of something shiny. Either silver or gold."

"I'll check to see if Alexander has anything we can use." She added another ornament to the branches in front of her.

"Hey, you can't just put all the gold ones together. You've got to mix up the colors. Spread them out. Put some deep inside the tree and some outside on the tips of the branches." He set his glass down and rose to join her, his swagger veering toward slightly tipsy.

"Who says? I doubt the Christmas police are going to come and issue me a fine."

Scoffing, he vaulted up onto the edge of the pot and started shifting some of the ornaments around. "I'll issue you the fine myself. It's an insult to holiday decorating."

"Be careful," she said through a laugh. "You already kissed the floor once today. I could be wrong, but being a scientist probably requires your brain matter to stay within your skull."

"I'm trying to correct your inferior tree decorating. There is holiday enjoyment at stake." He rose up on his toes and hooked on another ornament, teetering on the edge of the pot.

"Seriously, Liam. I can fly. I'll get the high ones. Don't hurt yourself. You're clearly suffering the effects of the wine."

"The wine... Yes, that reminds me, we should call for another bottle!" He shuffled around the side of the tree, circling his arms to catch his balance.

"Tribiscal wine is very strong, and you've had enough to slosh a dragon. I'm afraid if you have any more, I'll be carrying you to bed tonight."

He leaned into the tree, peering around the branches to look at her. "Promise?"

She laughed, feeling her cheeks grow warm. "I thought you said you wouldn't touch me again."

"We shouldn't. It will only make things more difficult."

She nodded slowly. "Right. We might develop an attachment to each other, after all. An infatuation perhaps, or something worse, like a genuine friendship."

He nodded his head. "Nothing good could come of it."

"You wouldn't want to give me the wrong idea. I might trap you if you're not careful. Refuse to take you home. Keep you here as my sex slave." She grinned wickedly and waggled her eyebrows.

His eyes narrowed. "I never thought of that. You wouldn't do that, would you?"

Men. She rolled her eyes. "Who says I'd want to? You seem like a lot of trouble. I'm not even sure you can do the job I brought you here to do. Those cookies were a disaster."

"They were, weren't they?" He snorted. "We shouldn't have left them behind. They belong disposed of in a bright red bag marked with a skull and crossbones." His laugh was cut off with a loud hiccup.

"Liam! You *are* drunk. By the Mountain, get down from there."

He walked backward along the edge of the pot, arms out.

"I'm not watching you." She hooked the basket of ornaments over her arm and lifted into the air, quickly decorating the top of the tree.

"Yes, you are," he said from below her. "You can't take your eyes off me. You haven't since the moment you brought me here."

"Done," she said, ignoring his outburst. She landed beside him and stared up at her handiwork. Stunning. It cast the entire room in a warm, colorful glow.

"Do you know how I know you haven't taken your eyes off me?" He blathered on, a hiccup punctuating his statement.

Annoyed, she looked up at him. "Mountain forgive me, I had no idea that humans couldn't hold their liquor," she murmured, wondering if she should call Maiara. Instead, she held up her hand. "Come down from there."

He slapped her hand away. "I know because I haven't taken my eyes off *you*. You're a fucking candle in the darkness. No man could look away from you."

Gods, he was far gone. She considered simply forcing him down but was afraid he might struggle and hurt himself. "All right then. Follow this candle and I'll put you to bed. You need to sleep it off."

"Who am I to deny a beautiful woman who wants to put me to bed?" Without warning, he jumped. Charlie broke his fall by grabbing his torso. The ledge was only about four feet high, but she worried he'd fall awkwardly and hurt himself in his current state. He landed against her chest, and she pushed him away, turning him toward the door. Truly, she didn't mind him touching her except that it reminded her of the orgasm he'd given her that morning and the idea that it wouldn't be happening again depressed her.

"You're a pain in the ass, you know that?" She nudged him forward with a light laugh.

"It's one of my finer qualities."

By the time they reached her chambers, she was practically holding him up. "Are you going to be okay? Maybe I should call Maiara."

"Fine," he mumbled. "Just very drunk."

"I can see that." She opened the door to her guest room and deposited him on the bed. He flopped onto the mattress, spread-eagle, and instantly closed his eyes. *Fuck.* He couldn't undress himself; she'd have to do it for him. One by one, she removed his shoes, then went to work on his fly. She glanced up at him as she undid the button and zipper on his jeans, but his eyes were closed. Thank the gods, because when she shimmied them down over his hips, she was sure she made a face when she saw what was underneath. Liam was hung like a mountain horse. She swallowed hard, cursing her luck for being attracted to a human with *that* body only to be rejected once again. She gritted her teeth and stripped the jeans from his legs, then covered him with the blanket.

She was draping the jeans across a chair when he said, "You know why those men reject you?" Fuck, was he reading her mind? "It's not because you have wings. It's because you're an angel. Good to your bones. The sum of everything light and beautiful in the world. No man can live up to that. You're too good for those fuckers."

"I don't think—" She started to tell him all the reasons that what he said wasn't true but stopped when he let loose a laborious snore.

Shaking her head, she slipped from the room and climbed into her own bed, alone again.

THIRTEEN

"Oww." Liam sat up, feeling like his head might explode. The events of the day before paraded through his mind, becoming ever foggier near the end when the tribiscal wine had kicked in. Damn, that stuff was potent. His gaze caught on his jeans hanging over the back of the chair. He lifted the blanket. Yep, she'd undressed him, and didn't that just intensify the morning wood he was sporting.

Just thinking about her hands on his fly had him palming his cock and stroking the rock-hard erection the vision gave him. The woman had him tied up in so many knots he was already anticipating weeks of recovery when he returned home and was forced to go cold turkey. Would he ever get over the softness of her feathers bunched in his fist, or the taste of her mouth, or the way her skin smelled like pure citrusy sunlight, and oh God, the light and heat she put off when she came? He stroked harder, faster. If he'd been buried inside her like he'd wanted to be, he might have lost his heart to her at that moment. Hell, he'd have given her his soul. As long as he lived, he'd never forget the moment she arched off the bed.

He jerked, tightening his hold on himself as the memory of her grinding against his palm pitched him over the edge. Hot jets streamed across his stomach. He lay there for a moment in the rosy glow of his fantasy before sounds outside the bedroom door sent him scurrying to the bathroom to clean up. Once he'd bathed and changed into another set of Alexander's clothes, he took his pounding head into the common area.

Charlie was waiting for him with a sympathetic smile. "This will help with that hangover." She poured what looked like water into a glass across the table from her.

"Thanks." He sat down and took a sip. Definitely not water. Tasted medicinal.

"I ordered a few dishes—scones, eggs, bacon." She lifted the silver domes off the plates. "I wasn't sure what you'd be in the mood for."

He stared across the table at her, thinking he was in the mood for her. Beating himself off that morning, it seemed, had only whetted his appetite. He shifted in his seat and started reciting the periodic table in his head, grabbing a scone off the platter. "I'm sorry about last night."

"That's all right," she said softly. "I should have warned you that tribiscal wine is strongly intoxicating. Most full-grown dragons don't drink as much of it as you did."

"What about your human relatives?"

"The ones who are witches don't drink it at all. One glass can knock a witch on her ass. My uncle Nick usually has a couple, but he's used to it."

He chewed his scone thoughtfully, the memory of what he'd said to her coming back to him. "What I said last night—"

"It was sweet."

"It was inappropriate. You don't need me opining on your romantic life." He took another sip of the concoction in his glass. "Frankly, I wonder if you need me at all anymore. You've got the tree and some decorations. The cookies are a bust. I think you can figure out the meal."

"Actually, both of those things are done." She reached behind her and grabbed a box off the desk. "It turns out my mother has an affinity for Earth cookies and Cook knows how to make them."

She thrust the pink box toward him, two perfect-looking chocolate chip cookies inside. He nabbed one and tried a bite. Not exactly the same as what he remembered from home, but far closer than he'd managed. "Delicious."

"She helped me come up with a menu based on my aunt's favorite foods. She swears they are all Earth inspired."

Why did Liam's chest feel like it was collapsing? "It sounds like you have everything under control then. So... will you be taking me back today?"

Although her lips bent into a smile, it didn't reach her eyes and her gaze lingered on the hot beverage in her hands. "I'm afraid it will have to wait. Dimension hopping is exhausting, and I have to lead a very important meeting today."

Too eagerly, he nodded. *Fuck, Liam, stop acting like a lovestruck teenager.* "Later is fine."

Now her eyes were on him, her smile broadening. The delay seemed to improve her mood and left him wondering if she was struggling with the same inconvenient feelings of attachment as he was. Ridiculous emotions considering their circumstances. He had to remember that.

"I should probably get going. Make yourself comfortable. Tonight we can talk more about getting you home." She stood and straightened the jacket on the silky pantsuit she was wearing.

"I meant what I said last night," he blurted. "I was drunk but not too drunk to know what I was saying." In his head, he kicked himself, furiously begging his mouth to shut the hell up. But for some reason, his heart and his brain wouldn't listen.

"You said a lot of things, Liam. You were extremely critical of my decorating skills." She slanted him a tight smile.

"I mean what I said about the men here. They must be intimidated by you. By your beauty and your intelligence. It's not the wings. They're just not man enough to handle someone like you. You unnerve them."

She cocked her head to the side. "Do I unnerve you?"

Sliding his thumb along his jaw, he shook his head. "No, ma'am. If we were from the same world, I'd have no problem keeping up with you. I'd enjoy every second of it."

Before she could turn away, he watched a gorgeous blush return to her cheeks. "But we'll never know for sure because we *are* from different worlds, and as you said before, we can't risk anything happening again, can we?"

Hearing his words thrown back at him was a blow to the chin. She was right of course, but fuck if he didn't wish she wasn't. "Right."

She grabbed a portfolio from her desk and slipped out the door without another word.

LIAM PEERED THROUGH A CRACK IN THE DOOR TO THE meeting room, completely enraptured by Charlotte's performance inside. She was leading something called the Elder Council. From what he'd gathered, ambassadors from each of the five kingdoms came together regularly in this meeting to resolve their disputes. He'd never taken an interest in politics, but he'd been standing there for over an hour, his feet growing sore, and he couldn't bring himself to leave. She commanded the room as well as any leader he'd ever observed, handling delicate matters with panache.

"While I can appreciate your predicament, Ambassador Hermecles, I'm not sure what role you'd like the kingdom of Paragon to play. Are you asking for direct assistance dealing with the snails or economic support while you address the issue?" She gave the ambassador from Rogos her full attention.

"Charlie's something else, isn't she?"

Liam whirled to find a terrifyingly large man standing behind him with ghostly white hair and silvery eyes. If there was any doubt he was a dragon, it was dismissed the moment Liam saw the two taloned, bat-like wings hulking over his shoulders. Adding to his strange appearance, tattoos of mysterious symbols covered his exposed skin, everywhere but his face. All the dragons he'd met so far had struck him as potentially deadly. This dragon looked as if he wouldn't just kill you but inhale your soul if he saw fit.

"Y-yes, she is," he said, finding his voice. "She's good at what she does."

"Apologies if I startled you. I am Marius, Charlie's uncle." *Another uncle.* "You must be Liam. My brother tells me you're helping her with a project." Marius's smile was friendly enough, if not exactly mollifying given his overall appearance.

"I am, although I think we're almost done."

"You'll be anxious to go home then."

Liam turned back toward Charlotte. Was he anxious to go home? No, he wasn't. His chest tightened at the thought. He should say something though. It was going to happen whether he wanted it to or not. He glanced back at Marius and nodded, "I've enjoyed my time here, but I'm sure my absence on Earth has left a mess."

"Charlie can help you clean that up. She's great at wiping minds."

Wiping minds? "Oh?"

"Yeah, she'll probably ask to wipe yours with your consent. Not that we have anything to fear from you talking. No one would believe you. But it might be easier for you. Keep you from thinking you hallucinated all this. In fact, I recommend it for your mental health."

The thought of Charlie erasing the past few days made his skin crawl. "I don't want my mind wiped. I can handle the memories."

Marius held up his hands. "Talk to her about it, not me. You're her mess. I could take you back but she's better at it. I can cross dimensions. She can travel time itself. She's very powerful."

"I heard one of her other uncles say she's not supposed to leave Paragon. Why is that?"

Marius scoffed. "Unbelievable. Which brother was that? Did he share the keys to the treasure rooms with you too?"

"There are treasure rooms?"

Marius's wings stretched and retracted with his annoyance. "It was Colin, wasn't it? He's good with military secrets but horrible with personal ones."

"He didn't really tell me anything specific. I just overheard him say she needed to be careful."

"Yes, she does."

When Marius didn't expound on the comment, Liam pushed. "Why?"

"It's not my story to tell."

"But it's unsafe for her. She'll be in danger when she takes me back?"

"Probably not. Not immediately anyway."

"You've got to give me more to go on than that," he gritted out. Would it hurt her to bring him back? Was Earth's atmosphere a poison to her? What had she risked to bring him here? But his biggest question was why? Why had she taken such a risk to throw a party?

Marius chuckled as if Liam's questions came from a curious toddler. "As I said, it's not my story to tell. If you want to know, you'll need to ask her." The dragon reached for the door. "I must excuse myself. Technically I'm supposed to be in there helping her even if she doesn't need it. A pleasure to meet you, Liam from Earth. Good luck... with whatever you choose to do next."

FOURTEEN

Charlotte wrapped up her meeting with the Elder Council and gathered her things from the desk, anxious to get back to Liam. But when she moved to rise, Marius nudged her arm.

"I met Liam."

She sat back down, trying to look innocent. She hadn't thought Marius even knew who Liam was. She hadn't mentioned her project to him or that she'd dimension hopped. "You did? When?"

"He was watching you through the door when I arrived."

"He was?" Charlotte had started the meeting, and Marius had joined halfway through. How long had Liam been standing there?

"He was." He threaded his fingers on the conference table. "He didn't seem excited about going back. Can you explain that?"

Leaning back in her chair, she sighed. "I have no idea. He seemed anxious enough to return home this morning."

"Oh? Because when I spoke with him, he seemed oddly protective of you."

She shook her head. "No. I don't think..."

Marius ran a thumb along one pale brow. "He wanted me to tell him why you're not supposed to leave Paragon."

"Did you?"

"No."

"Thank you."

"Why does it matter if I told him or not, Charlie?"

"I don't want him to worry about it."

"Why does it matter what he worries about when you promised you'd wipe his mind?"

She winced. "Alexander told you that, huh?"

"Yeah. And it's a good idea. Alexander told me this human is a scientist. He'll want to make sense of it. He could talk. Or obsess. Human minds are weak. If he talks, others might think he's mad, or he might go mad thinking about it."

"Human minds *aren't* weak. What about Nick? Avery? Clarissa? Mom? His mind isn't weak, Marius. I know I said I'd wipe his memories, but I won't do it without his consent. It's wrong."

He gave her a crooked smile. "Oh, Charlie."

"What?"

"You have feelings for him."

She scoffed. "Don't be ridiculous. I've known him three days."

"I fell in love with Harlow the first time I saw her." Marius's strange silver eyes turned reminiscent.

"She was your fated mate. That's different." She thought for a second. "And hadn't you met when she was a teenager? You didn't fall in love until after you were resurrected."

He leaned back in his chair. "In retrospect, I loved her in my own way."

She rolled her eyes at the exaggeration. "What is this about, Uncle?"

Leaning toward her, he took a deep breath. "I talked to the man for five minutes, Charlie, and I think he has feelings for you too."

She inhaled sharply. "I-I... It's impossible. He's going home in a matter of hours."

He scratched the back of his head. "I've lived a long, long time, and love—my love for Harlow and the kids—it's the best part. So if you get a chance at that—"

"That's not what this is."

"It's like you told me before. You're not a little girl anymore. You're a powerful woman. If you get a chance at something you want, take it."

"But—"

Marius cast one last smile in her direction and slipped out the door, his silver wings trailing behind him.

❄

CHARLIE FOUND LIAM IN HER CHAMBERS, STANDING ON THE balcony, his hands in the pockets of his borrowed jeans, watching Paragon's suns set behind the mountains. From the time he'd arrived, she'd become accustomed to the scowl that always seemed at home on his face. But she saw something else there now. A hint of sadness. No, something beyond sadness, something she couldn't quite place. Despair possibly. She wished she had the magic to read his heart, but as powerful as she was, that was something she couldn't do.

"I know you're probably anxious to get home, but if you're willing to wait until morning, I'd love to take you into Hobble Glen to shop for gifts to go under that tree."

He turned as if just noticing she was in the room. "I'd like to see Hobble Glen. Besides, I'm sure you're tired after today."

She wasn't, but she nodded anyway. "Tomorrow it is. Take a jacket. It gets cold when the suns set."

He didn't say another word until they were in the carriage. In fact, he hardly looked at her. "I met Marius today," he finally said, his gaze fixed on the window.

"He told me. Don't tell anyone, but he's my favorite uncle. We've always had a close relationship."

Liam licked his lips, and a charged silence unraveled between them. After some time, he said, "Is the offer still open, Charlotte? Will you tell me your secret if I tell you mine?"

She chewed her lip. What did it matter if she told him? In a day's time, she'd never see him again.

"Yes, the offer is still open."

Planting his chin in his palm, he cracked his neck. "You were right. There is a reason I didn't go to my father's funeral. A more personal reason than just a divisive position on the business."

"Whatever you tell me, I won't judge you. These things can be complex." She rested a hand lightly on his knee.

He placed his hand on top of hers, and she waited patiently while he gathered his words.

"When I went into the military, the Army accepted all my paperwork initially. But after a few months, I was called into an administrative office. There was a problem with my birth certificate." It must have been obvious that she didn't know what that was because he added, "That's an official Earth document that proves your parentage and where you were born." When she nodded her understanding, he said, "Mine was a forgery."

"What?"

"That's what I said. And the records keeper showed me how the document I had did not match up with the records from the county where I was born. There were other things. The certificate wasn't properly embossed with the county seal. They'd tried multiple times to get an official copy, thinking it was just a mistake, but there was no record of my birth... anywhere."

"Oh, Liam, that must have been confusing."

"That's the understatement of the year. I had no choice but to go to my mother to clear things up. But she couldn't. In fact, when I confronted her, things became far more complicated. She told me to drop it and offered to have their lawyers speak directly to records administration, but I couldn't let it go. I could tell she was hiding something. So I went to my father and asked him for the truth. He was never a kind-hearted man. Always the type that enjoyed the kill a little too much. He couldn't resist telling me the truth, and he made no effort to soften its sharp edges."

He stopped talking and rested his head against the back of the seat to stare at the roof of the carriage.

Charlie didn't want to push him, but she lifted from her seat and moved to his side of the carriage, taking his hand in hers. It was a tight fit with her wings, but she perched on the edge of the seat and waited in silence.

He took a deep breath before adding, "My father had an affair with one of our housekeepers. Actually, it was more than one, I'm sure, but this particular affair resulted in a pregnancy. My mother threatened to divorce him, but he held all her financial assets. He had complete control and a team of lawyers to back him up. And my mother had wanted a baby. I'm the oldest child. Spencer and Kara weren't born yet. So my dad came up with the idea of paying this poor woman to cut all ties with the outside world and deliver me in secret on Morris property. My family's private doctor delivered me, and Dad's lawyers created the fake birth certificate when the doctor refused to lie on the real one. After she delivered, my mom was paid off to never speak of me again and was released from her position."

Charlotte had to force herself to swallow. She couldn't imagine having a child effectively stolen from her arms. No wonder Liam carried such awful feelings about his father.

"By the time I knew her name, my real mother was dead, and so was the doctor who delivered me. No one else knew. Not even my siblings. And of course my dad said if I told anyone, he would deny it. His lawyers made a new birth certificate happen after the Army started sniffing around, this one registered correctly with the county. I have no idea how much that cost him."

"Gods, Liam, I'm so sorry." She squeezed his hand and wrapped one wing around his shoulders.

He finally met her eyes. "The worst part was that I lost both my parents that day. I despised my father for what he did, but I also lost my mother. Not because we didn't share the same genes. I didn't care about that. I lost respect for her. She'd lived with my father's cheating my whole life. It was so clear to me then, the things you remember as a kid but don't put together until you're older. And she'd gone along with his plan. She'd even made a photo album with staged pictures of a fake pregnancy and my first day home. The lie was... elaborate to say the least. And because of that, I never even had the chance to meet my own flesh and blood."

"No wonder you didn't choose to honor his death. How hard it must have been for you. He put you in a place where you had to redefine your identity and then abandoned you to do it on your own."

Liam nodded. "I'm sure you can understand why I don't like to share about this."

"I understand. Especially to someone like me whom you've only known a matter of days."

He snorted. "Days. It feels longer, doesn't it?"

She nodded slowly. "As if we've known each other for years."

"It's the strangest thing." Their eyes locked and held. When he finally looked away, he said, "I struggle, now that he's dead, with how involved I want to be with the rest of them. As complicit as she was, my mother had little control over the situation. She was at his mercy like everyone else. And my siblings didn't know anything at all. Maybe, now that he's gone, I should give them another chance. She requested I come this year for Christmas, said she had an important announcement. I'm considering it."

She studied him for a moment, heartbroken by the

sadness that seemed to plague him. "I can't possibly tell you what to do in this situation, Liam, but I know if you look into your heart, you'll find the right answer."

He nodded. The carriage came to a halt, and the driver opened the door.

"We're here," she said softly.

They exited into the streets of Hobble Glen, but he refused to release her hand. "As excited as I am to explore this town, you owe me a secret."

FIFTEEN

The village of Hobble Glen was something straight out of a Tolkien novel with slate-roof cottages and stone masonry. The layout reminded him distantly of Paris, with a central square and streets that branched off in a pie shape, the village circling out toward the mountains in the distance. But as quaint and fascinating as the architecture and civic layout was to Liam, his notice of it was fleeting. He was far more fascinated by the woman at his side.

Telling Charlotte he was the bastard son of a megalomaniac was something Liam had dreaded, but somehow he felt lighter having done so. In all his life, he'd never told anyone about his parents. The only one left alive who knew besides himself was his mother. But somehow, now that Charlotte knew, it felt more real, like this illicit story of his origins had meaning. It mattered, he realized. Over the years, the truth had begun to feel like something he'd made up, a vivid dream that he couldn't shake. Saying it out loud gave it credence, and he'd needed that more than he thought he did.

"My secret feels shallow now that I know what yours is," she said. "I almost hate to tell you for fear of trivializing your situation."

He yanked her to his side and smiled against her ear. "Oh no. You're not getting out of this that easily. I want to know no matter how trivial."

She stopped and took his face in her hands. "You know, I'd tell you a secret every day if I knew it would keep that smile on your face."

He had caught himself smiling more than usual since he'd been here. It was her, of course. She carried joy with her everywhere she went. You couldn't help but smile.

She tugged him forward through the crowded street. People were staring. Some acknowledged her with a shallow bow. Others turned away, whispering to each other. He had to force down the urge to take the latter by the throat and shake some respect into them. *Oh yes, the angel of Paragon is with a human. Get over it, fuckers.*

"My secret is this...," she began. "As you know, I'm different from others of my kind. I'm not a dragon like my father or a witch like my mother."

"So I gathered."

"I am a celestial being, the only one of my kind on Ouros."

"Got it." Where was she going with this?

"But I'm not the only one of my kind."

The streets were filled with shoppers, but he barely noticed the quaint stores around them. He gripped her hand tighter. "There are others like you, on other planets?"

"In other realms." She stopped to look inside the colorfully decorated window of what Liam assumed was a candy store. "When I was a child, I was once trapped inside one of the levels of the underworld. Marius came and got me out. Beings like me were guarding the gate. Well, not exactly like me. They were monsters. Unthinking. Unfeeling. Used to protect what the gods want to protect—in this case, Hades. They were called guardians."

"There are levels to the underworld?" His voice cracked, and Liam tried to keep it together.

"Yes. How you live your life determines where you go. I was trapped in a realm Marius called the Fire Planet, an awful place where it rains fire and monsters rule. It was the first time I ever had to use my defensive magic. I produced a shield against the guardians, and my uncle and I were able to escape."

"Thank God." Liam's heart thumped in his chest. He was not okay with picturing Charlie as a child being attacked by monsters in some hellscape.

"After we returned here, my mother did more

research into my kind. There wasn't much about us, but the scribes of Rogos eventually found a few ancient scrolls with information on what I was. She found out that dragons were once bred by the gods to produce guardians. You see, my mom, she's not just a witch—she's a descendant of the goddess Circe. I am not just part human witch and part dragon. The blood of a goddess also flows in my veins. Others like me are the product of gods and dragons, and they are enslaved into the protection of the god who created them."

Liam scowled. "But you are no slave."

"No, I'm not. My parents created me because they love each other. But I'm not supposed to leave Ouros because my parents are afraid that if I do something to attract the attention of the gods, one of them might come for me, try to enslave me. The gods won't respect my freedom. They could attempt to capture me and use me for their purposes."

He pulled her closer, as if there were anything he could do to protect her from the whims of the gods. Shit, he didn't even believe in God, singular or plural... until this week, he supposed. She wasn't lying to him, and he had to admit that after everything he'd seen and learned here, a higher power was a real possibility. His graduation from atheist to agnostic though didn't mean he was a fan of whoever was calling the shots, especially if they were a threat to Charlotte. Which made him wonder about something.

"If that's true, why don't they come for you here?"

She turned in his arms, her long fingers coming to rest on his chest, and stared up at him, her deep, fathomless blues drawing him in again. So trusting. So vulnerable. Great. Now he'd graduated from believing there could be a god to feeling like *he* was a god.

"This island is protected by the goddess of the mountain. She lives here, and when I am here, I am under her protection. She gave my parents her blessing. But if I leave here, I am beyond the reach of her defense."

He took a step back, her uncle's comments finally making sense. "You put yourself at risk when you came to get me?"

She sighed. "Theoretically. My parents are going off some old scrolls and folklore. The truth is that the gods are likely too wrapped up in themselves to know I exist or to bother with me. The chances that they'd detect me and go through the trouble of coming for me are very low."

"But possible."

"Yes, possible."

Liam tensed, pulling her closer. "Maybe you should have Marius take me back."

She laughed. "No. He can move between worlds but not back in time. I can return you to the precise moment I took you. He can't."

"That's important actually." If he didn't return to that moment, Noah would have already left and presumed he was dead. It would complicate everything immensely. And although Marius said she could wipe minds to undo those complications, she couldn't do that if she wasn't the one bringing him back.

"Are you okay?" she asked him.

"I don't want to forget you," he blurted. "Marius said you might wipe my mind. I want you to know that I don't want that."

She cupped his face. "Okay."

His stomach twisted at the thought of how little time they had left together. Here, now, with her in his arms, it all felt right somehow. She knew the truth about him, and she accepted it. She didn't care about money. Hell, she didn't even know why his last name mattered. He was no one here. No one but who he was to her. And at the moment, that was enough.

"I think the sharing of each other's secrets deserves some celebratory ice cream." She slid her hand into his.

"You have ice cream?"

"We do, although my mom says it's different than yours." She guided him to a street vendor where she ordered a cup of something that was fluorescent orange and tasted like mashed avocado whipped with chocolate. It wasn't horrible, but it wasn't what he thought of when he heard the words *ice cream*.

"Do you like it?" she asked around a bite.

He hesitated to answer, not wanting to dull the

mood. "I like eating it with you." Lord, he hated that it wasn't a line. He meant every word. This breakup was going to hurt.

She responded with a soft blush that melted his heart. "Will you help me pick out Christmas gifts for my family?"

"Sure."

Shop after shop, they chatted about traditional Christmas gifts: Nordic sweaters, sleds, gaudy Christmas ties. None of his ideas were appropriate for Paragon, but they found a lovely scented candle for her mother and a pair of gold cuff links for her father. Jewels, he learned, were so ubiquitous in Paragon as to be as inexpensive as plastic to its residents, but gold, which came from Nochtbend, was highly valuable.

"What do you think of this for my aunt Avery?" Charlotte asked, showing him an ankle-length duster that looked like it was made of silk but was as light as air to the touch.

"I don't know your aunt, but it seems like something a woman would like." He rubbed the fabric between his fingers. "I've never felt material like this."

"It's vilt. Very fine vilt. The woman who owns this store is one of a kind, a master weaver."

He dropped the edge of the garment. "As a princess, I'm surprised you don't have a closet full of this stuff."

"I could if I wanted it. I have a few pieces that I

wear when I need dignitaries to take me seriously. But to wear it all the time would be pretentious and potentially alienate me from the commoners of Paragon. I've always made it my goal to be approachable."

He shook his head, overwhelmed by feelings of respect for her. She'd told him she was twenty-five in Earth years, but it was clear to him that she was far more mature than any human woman he'd ever met. "I wonder if your parents know what they have in you? You're not just a princess, Charlotte, you're a leader, and a really good one. I hope that this Christmas thing does what you want it to do, because I think your parents have severely underestimated you."

She swallowed hard. "Thank you for that." She moved toward the checkout, placing the duster on the counter along with a tunic she'd already picked out for her aunt Clarissa. "Sometimes I think my family is just too close to see me clearly. Do you know what I mean?"

He nodded. "Yeah, I do." For some reason, his voice was all grit. God, his chest was going to collapse thinking about not being the one to see her when no one else did, to tell her exactly how magnificent she was every single day. He swallowed. "I see you, Charlie. And I feel lucky to know you. There's no one like you. Not anywhere."

A gorgeous blush stained her cheeks and she turned away quickly, her expression growing serious as she paid for the items with money he learned was called dragmars. He'd made a fool of himself admitting how he felt about her. The space between them seemed to widen, an awkward tension pressing into the room.

She grabbed the bags and hooked them over one arm. "I'm ready to go back to the palace."

Silently, he took her bags and walked her back to the carriage. Once they were alone inside and the wheels were turning toward home, she finally spoke.

"I don't think there's anyone like you either, Liam. I know you said you didn't want to touch me, that you were afraid to promise me something you couldn't deliver. What if I told you that I have no expectations? I know how this ends." She glanced down at her fingers, tangled in her lap. "And I still want you. We'll never get this time back. I just want to know what it's like to be with you before we have to say goodbye. Is that so bad?"

Liam couldn't believe what he was hearing, but his body could. His body was ready to give her what she wanted instantly. A lump formed in his throat, and his tongue seemed to swell to three times its normal size. The ice that had protected his heart when he'd arrived three days ago had long since melted, and there was nothing left between him and her besides his will and a few bags of Christmas gifts. He kicked the latter aside with his foot. As for his will, he wanted her. Was there a moment he hadn't? Was there a reason he shouldn't? He didn't remember. He didn't care to.

He slid onto the seat beside her and draped his hand across her knee. Casually, he stroked up the inside of her thigh with the backs of his nails. "Your wish is my command, Princess."

SIXTEEN

Charlotte stared at Liam beside her. Surely her body would combust. He wasn't scowling anymore. The only emotion she could read on his face was one of abject desire. And she was right there with him. A rush of heat gathered between her thighs, and she leaned toward him, her lips parting in anticipation. He didn't disappoint. He captured her mouth with his, his big body pressing against hers, perched on the edge of the bench.

She lost herself in that kiss. His tongue stroked hers, teasing, tempting. His fingers dug into her hair, their tug against her scalp a demand. Reaching up, she clasped the base of his neck, their kiss becoming almost brutal with their need. For the first time ever, she wished she were the type of woman to wear dresses. She wanted to straddle him, right there in the cab, have him inside her before her next breath.

As it was, the heady kiss ended when the carriage pulled to a stop. Liam broke from her, grabbing the packages and holding them in front of his hips before the driver opened the door. Charlie wiped a hand over her face, knowing the move probably wouldn't disguise what they'd been doing. The driver was a dragon and most assuredly could smell the lust coming off them. He'd likely notice her swollen lips too.

Lucky for both of them, the servants of the palace were known for their discretion. The driver barely looked their way as she stepped down behind Liam, and they strode side by side at a respectable distance into the palace. No one seemed overly concerned by their passage through the halls to her chambers either. Although they greeted a member of the housekeeping staff, she didn't say a word other than hello or give them so much as a sideways look. Still, she was relieved it was only the servants and not her uncles they ran into before slipping inside her chambers and locking the door behind them.

He dropped the bags on the sofa and stripped off the leather jacket he'd borrowed from Alexander, throwing it beside them. "Charlotte, if this isn't what you want, tell me now. I can hardly breathe—I want to be inside you so bad. Don't tease me if you've changed your mind."

In answer, she removed her boots and kicked them aside. "I haven't changed my mind. Have you?"

Approaching her, he shook his head, dug his fingers into her waistband, and sank to his knees, peeling her leggings off. He tossed them aside without ever looking away from her. Gods, the sight of his oversized body at her mercy ignited an electrical storm within her, a rush of heat gathering low. Muscles swelled below golden skin. Human he might be, but she felt fragile in his presence... small. His hands landed on her thighs, spreading her feet wider, his thumbs dusting over her slit.

"You are so wet for me, Princess." Mountain his voice was low, rough as burnt cinders. He ran a knuckle along her center. "Is that for me?"

"Yes," she rasped, unable to catch her breath. Her cheeks blazed. She'd never done anything like this with a man. Never had a man wanted this. But Liam did. She could smell his desire for her like a spicy musk in the air that made her heart pound.

"And your scent. Do you know how perfect you smell?"

She shook her head. She couldn't speak, not with him staring up at her like that. Gods, he ran his nose along the same path his knuckle had taken, coaxing a shaky breath from her lungs. Her breath wasn't all that was shaking. She trembled in his grip, wanting something she didn't know how to ask for.

"Like sunlight and citrus. I wonder how you taste." He licked up her center with the flat of his tongue, humming his approval. *That* was what she needed.

"Gods, do it again," she said softly.

He grinned up at her and did.

Without a doubt, although he was the one on his knees, she was the one under his control. Bracing herself on his shoulders, she tipped her head back and moaned as he licked her again, his tongue and teeth coaxing wicked currents of pleasure from her flesh. The tip of his tongue circled her clit, and she thought her soul might leave her body. That wonderful pressure was building like it had before, the base of her spine tingling with it.

Gods, when he speared her with his tongue, her trembling knees almost gave out. He held her up by her thighs as he increased his pace, licking, sucking, scraping her with his teeth, his beard grazing her skin, rough but delicious. Warm, wet, faster, harder. Golden light gathered around her, the feeling impossible to contain.

"God damn," he murmured against her as she arched her back and the light consumed her.

She was still writhing with the aftershocks when he scooped her up, wrapped her legs around his waist, and carried her into her bedroom.

"By the Mountain, Liam, I've never felt anything like that."

He lowered her to her feet at the end of the bed and started removing her top. It was a hip-length tunic, held in place by a corset that fastened beneath her wings. He turned her around to work on the strings, not at all hindered by her feathers.

"Good. Selfishly, I hope you never do again. Well, not with anyone else."

Over her shoulder, she saw the corners of his eyes wrinkle with his wolfish smile. He tossed her corset and the tunic underneath aside and spun her around, pushing her back on the bed. She went willingly, fanning her wings out beneath her naked body and watching him as he undressed. He fisted the back of his T-shirt and pulled it over his head.

She couldn't look away. Chiseled shoulders, broad and golden-skinned, met a chest with a smattering of dark hair that trailed over the peaks and valleys of his stomach to disappear inside his blue jeans. His eyes never left hers as he made short work of his fly and pulled both jeans and underwear down his legs.

Her heart pounded in her throat when he prowled onto the bed and positioned himself between her knees, his proud length jutting toward her, far larger than her previous lover. Massive. Beautiful. She gripped it in her hand, reveling in the way her touch made him sift air through his teeth.

"My god, Charlotte, I love it when you touch me."

"I don't have much experience. No experience with a human," she whispered.

He stretched over her, his eyes hooded. "I think we can figure it out."

His lips found hers again, and he settled between her thighs, her hand still gripping him between their bodies. She dragged the head of his cock along her slit, deepening the kiss as she lined him up with her entrance. A deep, satisfied sound left his throat as he pushed into her, met resistance, pulled out, and pushed in again.

"You're tight." He rested his forehead against hers.

"You're big."

His chest rumbled with his laugh, and then with one last thrust, he seated himself within her. "If you ever talk about me in the future, lead with that."

Charlotte had never felt closer to another person in her life. He drew her hands out to either side of her head and threaded his fingers into hers, showering her face and neck with soft kisses, worshipping her. Slow, so slow, he moved in and out of her, rocking his hips and stoking the fire between them. She melted under him, conforming to his body, her wings wrapping around both of them and brushing his back even as her fingernails scraped along his spine.

The pressure started again, made stronger by the way her heart pounded every time he stopped to look into her eyes or squeezed her fingers against the mattress. She bucked her hips against his, chasing the feeling that was just out of reach. She wanted more.

"Liam, faster."

He buried his face in her neck, growling as he picked up speed until his thrusts became sharp and punishing. She matched him hip to hip. The tingle strengthened, then exploded along her spine, her body arching off the mattress as light pulsed through her skin. He cried out and withdrew, his orgasm taking hold as warm jets coursed along her belly.

Pressing his forehead to hers, he panted into the space between them. She was panting too, her heart pounding, her soul still reaching for him. They stayed like that for a time, silent but somehow completely in sync, her heart beating in time with his. Her eyes flicked down to the mess he'd left on her belly.

"I'll get something to clean you up."

She almost cried out when he lifted off her and cold air filled the space where he'd been. He was only gone for a minute before returning with a wet towel, but it felt like an eternity. After, he cuddled against her, spooning her from behind, nestled between her wings.

"Liam?"

"Yeah?"

"That was more than I ever expected."

"From a human?"

"From anyone."

He sighed into the back of her neck.

"Hey, Liam?"

"Yeah." His voice sounded sleepy.

"Do you want to stay one more day?" She held her breath. It was bold to ask someone to give up another day of their life for something that couldn't possibly go anywhere.

She felt him press his forehead between her shoulder blades. Heard him swallow. "One more day."

She smiled into her pillow. "Good. I want to take you on a cruise of the Sanguine River. Maybe we can go to Rogos to see the snail migration. It's a huge problem for them but a magnificent thing to behold."

"You're a magnificent thing to behold," he murmured into her back.

She snorted. "You can't spend the entire day staring at me."

"Challenge accepted. I can. Watch me." He kissed the back of her neck. "As far as I'm concerned, we can spend the entire day exploring this bed and each other."

"Tempting," she said softly. Her lids felt heavy, the weight of sleep calling to her. She couldn't remember the last time she wanted to sleep. She went through the motions each night, but her body didn't need much and she rarely felt tired. But now, with Liam's arm around her, feeling warm and wanted, she couldn't fight its seductive tug.

She was almost asleep when she heard Liam whisper, "There are eight planets in Earth's solar system, one hundred billion in our galaxy, but if there was one person I could love in all the universe and the realms within it, it would be you, Charlotte."

His breath evened out and so did hers, and she allowed herself to sleep.

CHARLOTTE STARTED AWAKE TO THE SOUND OF A DRAGON'S growl and a cold draft where Liam's body once was. With one beat of her wings, she opened her eyes and leaped to her feet, horrified to find her father dangling Liam by the neck at the end of her bed.

"Dad! Stop! Put him down!"

"Who the fuck is this, Charlie? And talk fast before I crush his throat."

"He's my..." What in Hades should she call him? Lover? Friend? "Boyfriend."

Gabriel released Liam with a groan. He dropped roughly to the floor and crumpled into a ball, wheezing. She rushed to his side and wrapped a wing protectively over him.

"For Mountain's sake, put some clothes on," Gabriel groused.

She snatched her robe off the post at the foot of her bed where she often kept it, then pulled a blanket off the bed to wrap around Liam before handing him his clothes. "Bathroom," she whispered. "Let me handle this."

He gave her a nod, still massaging his throat, and slipped off, closing the door behind him.

Her father's burning gaze followed Liam until the door closed, then redirected on her. "He's human. How, may I ask, did you come by a human 'boyfriend'?"

"I brought him here to help me with a party I'm throwing for Aunt Avery. I wanted an Earth holiday theme."

"Christmas," he growled. "I saw the tree in the great hall."

She nodded.

"So how did he go from party planner to naked in your bed?" he said through his teeth.

She lowered her chin. "That part just happened."

He scoffed. "Fuck, Charlie. You've got to learn to make better decisions."

For a moment she was speechless, but when she found her voice, there was an edge to it. "Better decisions?"

"You can't jump into bed with every being that looks in your direction!"

The words hit her like a slap, and she took a step back. "I didn't *jump into bed* with anyone, but if I did, it would be my business. It's my body. I'm an adult and I'll do with it as I please." She'd never defied her father outwardly like this before, but she couldn't stand one more second of this high-handed conversation.

He growled down at her, baring his teeth, his chest rising and falling with his anger. King Gabriel was an imposing presence. When she was younger, he could stop her dead in her tracks with a hard look. But she stood up straighter now, her power crackling in the air around her. She would not be shamed for what she'd done last night. The memory of it was still a warm sun, glowing in her heart. She wouldn't change a thing for all the dragmars in Paragon and certainly not because of her father's censure.

"I have feelings for him, Father, and I don't regret a thing. You owe him an apology."

"That won't be happening." He scowled. "You do know you can't keep him, right? He's not a puppy. You can't just pluck a human out of his daily life and drop him in Paragon to be your plaything."

She winced. "Of course not. That's not how it was."

"So you left Paragon without our permission, despite our warning to you that it could be dangerous."

"I was only gone a matter of minutes."

"And you brought a stranger from another world into our palace even though you knew it could be a security risk."

"He's no threat to us or anyone else."

"When does he go back?"

"Tomorrow." Charlie gritted her teeth. "What are you even doing here? I didn't think you were supposed to be back for weeks."

"Obviously," he drawled, his disapproving gaze sliding down his nose at her. "The spell worked. We're in the waiting period until Nathaniel and Queen Penelope feel it can safely be reversed—two weeks. But your mother is already crawling the walls. I came to collect some novels from the library for her and her sisters to distract them from the wait."

"Tell them I love them," she said, relieved he would be going back.

"You need to come with me. I'm not leaving you here alone after this."

She bristled. He couldn't be serious. "What are you talking about?"

"I come in here to see how you are and find you naked in bed with a stranger—"

"He's not a stranger!"

"Ruining yourself with someone who shouldn't even be here."

"How was I ruining myself?" But she knew what he meant. Traditionally, as princess, she was supposed to remain modest if not virginal to increase her chances of a suitable match. But not only was that philosophy antiquated and misogynistic, she was different. It wasn't like she had leagues of interested suitors pounding down her doors.

Her father held himself like the warrior he was. Was he actually trying to intimidate her over this? "You know very well how. It's clear to me that you're not old enough to make good choices, Charlie. I'm taking you back to Darnuith with me where I can keep an eye on you. Marius can take over here in our absence."

"I'm not going anywhere," she snapped. "I need to take Liam back."

He pointed his finger at the ground between them. "Then take him back NOW! I'll meet you in the great hall in thirty minutes."

In all her years, Charlie had never seen her father so angry or felt such hatred for how he was acting. Once, when political ties with Nochtbend were especially stressed, he'd raised his voice like that in a meeting, but she'd never had that anger directed at her, not even when she'd accidentally set the dining room on fire as a child. As he tore from the room, her stomach clenched with grief over the interaction. He was wrong. What had happened between her and Liam was meant to happen. She'd wanted it. It was the best night of her life. And as much as she loved her father, she hated him for ruining it.

Dressing quickly, she met Liam in her bathroom. "I really wanted you here for one more day, but I'm afraid we have to go."

He nodded, keeping his distance. All the walls she'd so carefully deconstructed it seemed were back in place. "It's all right. I'm ready."

SEVENTEEN

At thirty-eight years old, Liam had experienced more than one awkward situation where he was caught in bed with a woman. The first was at seventeen when his girlfriend's mother walked in on them. The second was an angry ex-husband. But he could count this as a first. Having a man the size of a dump truck yank him out of bed by the scruff of his neck and shake him like a rag doll was an experience he never wished to repeat even if leaving Charlotte was going to break his heart.

"I'll take you back to the exact moment I brought you here. It'll be like this never happened."

Like it never happened, he repeated in his head. They'd moved to her ritual room where he'd changed into his base layer and she was helping to fasten him into the big red suit. He put on his helmet before he was tempted to kiss her goodbye. It would only make things worse. He already felt like someone had reached down his throat with a giant pair of forceps and was trying to extract his heart through his mouth. His skin hurt every time he thought about never seeing her again. The only thing he could do was refuse to think of it and focus on returning to the work he'd left behind.

Helmet on, he brought his equipment back up. Oxygen ninety-nine percent. Temperature normal. Heart rate within range. "I'm ready," he said, finding a spot on the floor to concentrate on. Anything to keep from looking at her.

Inside the symbol at the center of the room, she spread her hands and a window elongated between them. Through it, he could see his rover, headlights glowing in the snow. She adjusted her hands and there he was. This was the moment in time when she'd arrived.

She linked her arm with his, her touch miserably unfelt thanks to the padding of the suit. The window grew larger. She stepped forward, and seconds later he was standing on the ice, in the headlights of his Arctic rover.

"Liam, you there, buddy?" Noah said into his intercom.

Frantically he turned until he could see her face through his visor and the tear that cut a glistening trail down her cheek, somehow defying the freezing temperatures.

"Goodbye, Liam," she mouthed.

"It happened," he yelled, reaching for her. "It happened!" *I love you*, he added in his head although that couldn't be true. He hadn't known her long enough to love her. He swallowed the words down.

She took one step back and then another, nodding and mouthing, *it happened*. Then she was gone.

"What happened, dude?" Noah said. "Do you need a rescue?"

Tears flowed wet against his cheeks. He couldn't control them and had no way to wipe them away. He let them drip onto the neck of his suit. "I'm fine, Noah. I'll explain when I get back. I'm on my way."

Two weeks later, Liam arrived in Chicago with his ice samples in tow and a giant chip on his shoulder. It hadn't taken much to convince Noah and the rest of the team that he'd seen a formation in the blowing snow that looked exactly like a person. They'd laughed at his mental hiccup, teased him mercilessly, but ultimately gotten back to work fast enough. They'd evacuated base camp and returned home, and he stowed his ice samples in the university lab where he intended to continue his research before returning to his efficiency apartment in Lake View.

But as he pushed through the door to his home, the interior felt as cold as the Arctic he'd just left. He'd lived here for years but never noticed how empty it was. He dropped his bags on the bed and sat on the edge, missing Charlotte to the marrow of his bones. Maybe he should get a dog. Maybe he should see a therapist. Maybe he should take up drinking. He stared in the direction of his galley kitchen, eyeing the bottle of bourbon on top of his refrigerator. It was a Christmas gift from a fellow professor he'd helped with some research. He'd never opened it.

He strode across the apartment and swiped it from its place, brushing the dust off the bottle. Opening it, he poured himself a glass. *Fuck*, he didn't want bourbon. He wanted tribiscal wine. He drank more. It wasn't satisfying, but he was willing to bet it could numb what was happening in his head.

Three knocks came on his door. Probably Mrs. Thornton from down the hall, bringing him his mail. Groaning, he slid the glass onto the table and padded over to open it.

Charlotte stood in the hall, only it couldn't be Charlotte. This person had no wings and was wearing human clothing.

"Hi," she said, and he thought his legs might buckle when it truly was her voice.

"Hi," he managed. "What happened to—?"

She held a finger to her lips and pointed inside his apartment. He stepped aside, opening the door wider for her. Then he closed and locked the door behind her, as if that lock could keep her there.

"I used magic to hide them," she said, pointing toward where her wings once were. "So that I could come see you. I should tell you that in my timeline, I left you only minutes ago. I used magic to find when you'd be in Chicago. I only stopped in Paragon long enough to take some of my mother's human clothes. I know it's been longer for you."

"Two weeks."

"I had to wait until you were back."

He had so many questions. They should talk, he knew. Communication was important. But at the moment, words wouldn't come to him. He settled for showing her exactly what he was feeling. He crashed into her, melding his mouth with hers and shuffling her back against the wall where he pressed himself into her. She released a gentle sigh into his mouth and wrapped her arms around his neck. Only when she was thoroughly kissed did he pull back.

"How did you find me?"

"Magic... and Google. There are twelve Liam Morrises in this city but only one lives in Lake View."

He brushed her hair back from her face. "I'm so glad you came, but what are you doing here? I thought your father—"

"I don't care what my father wants, Liam. I know what I want, and I want to be here. So I dropped you off at the North Pole and returned to Paragon, changed into this, and then dimension walked here." She fisted her hands between them. "All my life I've done what they asked me to do. I've gone along with everything, obeyed their every command, because nothing was that important to me. Their way or my way, it didn't make a difference."

Her eyes met his. "But you matter, and when I tried to tell my father that, he wouldn't listen. And all at once it just hit me. I'm an adult with the power to go anywhere I want. I can travel through time and space. And with all that power at my fingertips, the only place I wanted to be was here... with you."

His heart leaped even as warning bells went off in his mind. They'd only known each other a short time, and if what the legends said was true about the gods wanting to enslave her, she was at risk coming here. But he couldn't bring himself to bring up either of those things. She was here, in his arms, and he was going to appreciate every moment of it.

A low rumble sounded between them. "Was that your stomach or mine?"

"Mine," she said. "I haven't eaten today. I could have, when I first arrived here, but I was too nervous."

"About what?"

"Afraid you would reject me." She chewed her lip, looking as vulnerable as he'd ever seen her.

He scoffed and shook his head. "Never. But I don't have any food in the house. What do you say to a trip to the grocery store? We can make dinner here, watch a movie?" Taking her out to dinner was out of the question. He wanted her to himself tonight, both to keep her safe and so she could let out those pretty wings she had bottled up inside her.

"A movie?" She squinted, and he marveled again at the lack of technology in Paragon.

"Like live theater but they record it so you can watch it later. You have live theater, don't you?"

"Yes, but why would you record it?"

"Sometimes to save money. Other times for convenience. With movies you can watch whenever you want."

"Why wouldn't you want to watch it while it was happening?"

"Give it a chance. I think you might like it."

He slipped his down coat over her shoulders, then grabbed an old one he rarely wore from the closet.

"I don't need this," she said. "I can't feel the cold."

"It's twenty-seven degrees out there. You need it or some bighearted Chicagoan is going to try to take you to a women's shelter."

She threaded her arms through the sleeves, and he took her hand and tugged her toward the door. An hour later, Liam's stomach was threatening to eat him from the inside out and they'd just made it back to the apartment. Although he had all the fixings for chicken vesuvio, he was starting to regret not ordering a pizza instead. He'd never expected it would take so long to get through the grocery store, but Charlotte's constant stream of questions from how chickens were raised to where potatoes were grown had slowed their visit to a snail's pace. Then he'd spent ten minutes showing her cow pictures on his phone, then another ten minutes explaining the phone.

"You can let your wings out," he said while he jabbed buttons to preheat the stove. He wasn't a great cook, but this was a recipe he could handle.

"What about the windows?"

"In this city, no one will think twice about it."

She laughed, digging a red pepper out of the bag and biting into it like an apple. The yummy sounds she made told him she enjoyed it.

"We should probably wash that off first."

"Why? I can't catch anything."

He stared at her for a beat and then reached out to pull off the produce sticker. To his horror, she popped the pepper—stem, seeds, and all—into her mouth. She'd swallowed it before he could say anything. "I guess there's no point in washing it then."

He turned back to the stove and heated up some oil in his brazier before quickly chopping some potatoes.

"Why will no one think twice about it if I let my wings out in here? Are there other people with wings?"

He glanced back at her to see she still had them away. "Sort of. Cosplayers. Victoria's Secret models. The occasional drag queen. It's hard to see into my windows from the street, but people won't question it if you're inside anyway." He added the chicken to brown.

"I don't know what any of those things are but I

trust you." Her wings unfurled, sending his blood pulsing in his veins again and filling up his tiny kitchen with feathers. One landed in the pan, and he picked it out with his fingers.

"Sorry," she said.

He chuckled. "It's fine."

As soon as everything was browned, he slid it all into the oven and set the timer.

"How did you learn to cook?" she asked.

He shrugged. "You pick it up living alone as long as I have. But I wouldn't say it's my strong suit. I have about ten dishes I can make without setting off the smoke alarm."

"I've never cooked my own food," she said sadly.

He did a double take. "Really? Never? Not even a scrambled egg?"

She shook her head.

"Hmm. Well, today is the day." He reached into one of his cabinets and produced a glass bowl.

"What's that for?"

"While the chicken is cooking, we're going to make chocolate chip cookies. I cannot have you thinking those monstrosities we produced in Paragon are anything like the real thing.

"Those cookies were an insult to the word *cookie*."

"That just means we know how not to do it. There's no place to go but up." He grabbed the bag of chocolate chips and the butter he'd picked up and the sugar and the flour from the cabinet.

Together, they followed the instructions, but he let her do all the work. She packed the brown sugar, beat in the eggs, measured the vanilla. When the dough was done, he scooped some onto his finger and held it out to her.

"Aren't we supposed to cook it first?"

"You recently reminded me that you can't get sick, so trust me, you don't want to miss this."

She leaned forward and sucked it off his finger, making him forget all about how hungry he was.

"Mmm."

"Yeah." God, if he weren't half-starved, he'd bend her over the counter.

It grew silent for a second as he warred with his fantasies and decided to be a decent human being and feed her before he tried to get her back in bed. Sighing, he opened a bottle of prosecco and poured them both a glass.

"Liam, is it okay that I'm here?"

He took a sip of his wine and then handed her the other glass. "Yeah, it's okay."

"But what about what you said about not being someone who can do relationships? I'm completely in your space here."

He frowned. "How long were you intending to stay?"

She chewed her lip. "I don't want to be there anymore. I felt like a prisoner. The way my father treated you the morning he found us, it just made me see how little he respects me as an adult. I felt suffocated. But I left before I considered your feelings. I'm sure I can stay with my uncle Tobias if you don't want me here."

He took another sip of his drink, knowing what he wanted to say but afraid to say it. It was crazy. This was all crazy. "I'm glad you came. Maybe we should take it one day at a time though. For both our sakes."

She nodded. "Right. Of course."

"What do you think the odds are that your dad will bust down my door and dangle me out the window by my neck?"

"Zero for the next two weeks. I traveled through time to get here. His reality is two weeks in the future. And while my mother would be able to reach me using magic if she had any, he can't, and she won't have her powers back for at least fourteen more days. That's part of the spell they're doing in Darnuith. It would be a lot to explain."

He waved a few fingers. "No, I think I get the gist." He released a relieved breath. "Okay. It just so happens I'm on winter break from teaching these next two weeks."

"You are? Oh, because your Christmas is coming up."

He nodded. "Saturday."

"You don't have a tree." She looked around the tiny apartment.

"I don't usually observe the holiday."

She stopped to scrutinize him. "You don't celebrate Christmas, but you stayed in Paragon to help me throw a Christmas party?"

He nodded once. "I was interested."

"In Paragon?"

He lifted the corner of his mouth. "And you." God, he loved it when she blushed. He pulled out a cookie sheet and showed her how to space out the blobs of dough.

She did so, sipping her wine between rows. "I can't believe I went to the North Pole and found the one human who didn't celebrate Christmas."

He snorted. "There's more than one." A rogue thought entered his mind, and as much as he wanted to push it aside, he found he couldn't. There was one place he could take her where she could experience a real Christmas. He owed her that. He cleared his throat. "Actually, I think I mentioned to you that my mother has requested I come home for Christmas this year. She, uh, left several messages this week. There's some big announcement. She wants all of us to be there."

"Oh... Are you going to go?" She didn't look at him. Just like Charlotte. She was leaving room for him to go alone. Hell no. That wasn't what he had in mind.

"Why don't you come with me? My mom throws a traditional Christmas every year. You can see firsthand what it's like, I can find out what this big announcement is, and you can... meet them."

She stopped spooning cookie dough. "You want me to meet them?"

He sighed. "No, not really. I'm actually worried you might think less of me once you see what my family is like, but I don't want to go alone. I need you, to be honest."

Her brow furrowed. "Then you have me. And I won't judge you by what they're like. Not any more than you judged me for my father's behavior."

"Fair enough." The timer went off, but he couldn't find the potholders.

"I got it." She pulled out the pan with her bare hands.

He shook his head. And to think he hadn't believed in magic.

"I've never been so full in my life," she said, leaning against his shoulder with her legs pulled under her. They'd gorged themselves on chicken, then followed up with chocolate chip cookies that they'd both enjoyed far more than the ones they'd attempted in Paragon. She'd eaten four by the time he'd finished one. "Earth food is phenomenal."

"It can be. Some of it is shit. I wouldn't eat sushi from a gas station."

"No gas station sushi. Got it. Considering I don't know what either of those things are, I think I'm safe."

He kissed the side of her head and clicked the remote. "Movie time."

"What's this play called?"

"*Elf*. I think you'll like it. It's about an elf who travels from the North Pole to New York on a quest to find his real father."

"He doesn't know who his father is? How sad."

He grinned as the story started to unfold, and soon Charlotte was laughing hard enough to shake the couch. He barely followed what was happening on-screen. He couldn't take his eyes off her. Since the moment she'd walked in the door, all he could think about was having sex with her again, but for some weird reason, he didn't want to act on that impulse tonight. After examining the strange, dichotomous thoughts, he came to the conclusion that he wanted her to know he liked her for more than that. He wanted her to feel safe with him. To feel at home.

Fuck, he had it bad for this girl.

"Is everything okay?" she asked him.

"Yeah. Why?"

"You're frowning during a funny part." She blinked those impossibly blue eyes at him.

He glanced at the screen to see Will Ferrell being pummeled by Peter Dinklage and chuckled. "Sorry, I was thinking about something else."

"What?"

"Work." Okay, so he'd been thinking about her and what it meant that he was more concerned with when she'd have to leave than how long she'd be here. He didn't have to tell her that though.

"I don't believe you," she said. "I can tell when you're lying because your ears don't move."

Now he laughed outright. "My ears don't move?"

"When you force yourself to smile but don't mean it, they stay exactly the same. What were you really thinking about?"

"Do you think you're safe here?"

"You mean from the gods?"

He nodded. It wasn't what he was originally thinking about, but he hoped his genuine concern would show in his... ears.

"I think so. Honestly, I've always believed the fear was unwarranted."

"Maybe I should seek out the head of Medusa just in case."

"Can't. Athena fused it to the face of her shield," she said flatly, clearly not realizing he was joking. She leaned her head back on his shoulder. "Don't worry about it, Liam. If the gods come for me, I'll jump back to Paragon if I have to, but I doubt I'm in any danger. How would they even know I'm here?"

He kissed the side of her head and hoped to God she was right.

She was asleep by the time the movie ended, and he carefully scooped her into his arms and carried her to bed where he tucked her in, wings and all. He used the bathroom, then stripped down to his boxers before climbing in beside her.

He was very close to sleep when he heard her mumble, "Even if the gods do come for me, being here with you, for as long as it lasts, will be worth it."

EIGHTEEN

The Morris estate was just as Liam remembered. The massive Greek Revival home loomed on a hill overlooking the security building where he'd stopped at the gate in his electric rental car.

"Name?" The security guard, a black woman with a name tag that read Ruby, looked as if she was disappointed to have to work over the holidays. She addressed them without a hint of a smile.

"Liam Morris."

She flipped some papers on a clipboard. "Your name is on the list, Liam, but I don't see any clearance for a guest. What's your name, ma'am?"

"Charlotte," she said.

"Last name?" Ruby said, obviously annoyed.

Liam widened his eyes at her. Did she even have a last name? No one in Paragon seemed to, and he'd never thought to ask.

"Tanglewood," she said with an easy smile.

Ruby typed something into her computer.

"She's not on the list," Liam said. "I forgot to tell my mother I was bringing her, but if you—"

"Mrs. Morris just approved her. Welcome, and Merry Christmas."

"You too." Liam frowned as the wrought iron gate in front of the car opened. He hadn't told his mother he was coming. He'd hoped she'd be welcoming to Charlotte, but he didn't want to get his hopes up. He proceeded along the winding drive at an easy pace, procrastinating the inevitable confrontation.

"Oh, this is beautiful!" Charlotte's eyes widened at the swags of greenery, white twinkle lights, and enormous red bows that lined each side of the drive along with the occasional animatronic Santa Claus or reindeer constructed out of white lights. It was all professionally done and incredibly sophisticated, of course. The Morris estate would never settle for anything less.

"How long has it been since you talked to your mother?" Charlotte asked, not taking her eyes off the decorations.

"Since the day she called me to tell me my father died. August."

"How long since you've seen her in person?"

"A year. I spent a couple of hours with her here last Christmas."

He glanced over to see her watching him. She was stunning in the purple sequined dress and cashmere coat he'd bought her for the occasion. He'd never really appreciated women's clothes before, but the woman at the department store had outdone herself with this number. Or maybe Charlotte was just the type of woman who could knock you dead wearing a potato sack.

He pulled around the fountain in the circle drive and put the car in park, tossing the keys to the valet before rounding the car to open her door and help her out. When he turned back around, his mother was on the porch, waiting for them.

CHARLOTTE GAZED AT THE WOMAN WHO STOOD AT THE TOP of three short stairs in front of a sprawling building that reminded her of the homes in the Firedrake District of Paragon, and one word came to mind —*formidable*. This woman was no meek housewife or docile mother figure. She held herself like a queen. Fitting then that the house behind her was a type of castle. No wonder Liam had compared himself to a prince.

The Morris matriarch was as tall as her son and had a slender build, her beaded green jacket providing a sophisticated topper to a black silk jumpsuit and matching shoes sporting bright red soles. Her neck, ears, and fingers dripped with gold and emeralds that would have fit in easily in Paragon, and her pure white hair—as white as Marius's—was cut short on the sides and spiky on top. Gray-blue eyes peered out from behind thick, circular black glasses. They were so different from Liam's light brown eyes, but then Charlotte reminded herself that they weren't related by blood.

"Isn't this an unexpected treat," she said through bright red lips. "When Ruby messaged me to say my son was here with a guest, I assumed you'd reunited with Victoria."

Charlotte shifted uneasily, jealousy wrapping her in its prickly grip. Victoria must be the woman Liam mentioned he'd been engaged to previously. Was their relationship truly that serious that his mother would assume they'd be together again? *Don't be silly*, she told herself. *She's simply the last woman Liam was known to be with.*

She stepped forward and extended her hand in the way she'd seen other humans do. "Hello, I'm Charlotte... Tanglewood."

The woman scowled and kept her own hands in her pockets. Charlotte glanced inquisitively toward Liam, her smile fading. Did she do it incorrectly?

"You'll have to excuse me, dear. I don't shake hands since the pandemic. Can't be too careful about germs."

Charlie stuck her hands in her coat pockets and gave her a nod.

"Charlotte, this is my mother, Anne," Liam said when she didn't introduce herself.

"But please call me Mrs. Morris until we get to know each other better."

Charlotte tried to keep her expression neutral at the rude and unfriendly greeting. Mrs. Morris didn't seem to care what she thought, however. She reached into her jacket and withdrew a gold case, removing a slim white cylinder from inside.

"A cigarette, Mom? Really? You've taken up smoking now?" Liam's voice held a note of derision.

"At my age, dear, what does it matter?" She lit the end of the cigarette and drew the smoke deep into her lungs.

"I've always thought of the scent of my Uncle Nathaniel's pipe quite fondly," Charlie said, grasping for anything positive to say that might win the approval of this woman who clearly did not like her.

Mrs. Morris blew out a stream of smoke and stared down her nose at her. "Tanglewood, you say. Are you of the Connecticut Tanglewoods?"

She shook her head. "New Orleans."

"Hmm." She circled her cigarette in the air and sighed. "Please come in. Spencer and Kara are already here." With that, she turned on her heel and strode into the house.

When Liam took her hand, she pulled him to her side. "I'm sure she's just processing all the feelings she has, seeing you after all this time."

Liam did a double take. "What do you mean?"

"Why she's treating us so coolly."

Chuckling under his breath, Liam's eyes crinkled as he said, "That was her on her best behavior."

"Very funny."

"I'm serious, Charlotte," he whispered without a hint of humor in his voice now. "That's what she's always been like."

Charlotte cringed. She tried to picture that woman raising a child and couldn't. Surely she wasn't always like that.

Liam led her through an airy foyer where a man dressed in a black-and-white uniform took their coats before leading them into a room with a Christmas tree decorated in silver and white. In fact, the entire room was composed of white furniture and chrome fixtures, including the floor, which was white marble identical to what was in her mother's ritual room. Natural light brightened it all thanks to a wall of windows. Charlie had nothing against white, but this room looked like no one had ever been in it before.

"Come say hello to your brother." Mrs. Morris pointed her cigarette at a chubby, balding man in a red sweater.

He popped out of one of the chairs, his blue eyes widening when he noticed her. He slapped a thick hand into Liam's. "Liam, buddy. Nice to see you again. Who's this?"

"Spencer, this is Charlotte. Charlotte, my younger brother Spence."

"A pleasure to meet you," Charlotte said, trying the hand trick again. Thankfully he shook it, although she was repulsed by his sweaty palm. To her surprise, he kept hold of her hand and kissed the back. She turned wide eyes on Liam.

"You've outdone yourself with this one, little brother. She is an absolute angel."

Charlie snorted, unable to hold it in, and tore her hand away, not sure what to say.

Liam glared down at his brother, who was a good two inches shorter. "Are Katherine and the kids joining us today?"

Spencer cleared his throat. "Katherine and I are spending some time apart. It's temporary. Sorting out a few things. She has the kids at her mom's this year."

"You cheated on her. What did you expect?" Mrs. Morris blew smoke out of the corner of her mouth.

Charlie stiffened, embarrassed for the man. Whether it was true or not, he didn't deserve to have it shared with a stranger in that way.

"We're working it out, Mom. We're in counseling."

Mrs. Morris turned those icy blue eyes on Charlie. "I think all this marriage counseling crap is just a scheme to part a fool from his money. What marriages need today is a man to be a man and a woman to be a woman. It's time you man up and rein her in, Spencer. Tell her she won't get a dime if she divorces you. You'll hire a team of lawyers who will bury her so deep in paperwork she'll never be free anyway."

"Jesus, Mom," Spencer mumbled.

"Your father and I never went to counseling, Spencer. Roger was a man who knew how to lead a household. There's no reason adults can't have their own lives, but once you marry into this family, you stay married to the family."

Liam stiffened beside her, and Charlotte squeezed his hand supportively. He turned her toward the bar. "Let's get a drink."

Charlie wiped her palm on her dress and nodded. She wondered if it was hard for him to remain silent when his mother spoke about his father in those terms. This family was strange. In Paragon, she would have thought they hated each other based on the energy in the room. She hoped she wasn't contributing to the tension. Maybe coming today was a bad idea.

They hadn't even made it to the bar when a woman strode in from the hall and stopped directly in front of them. She didn't have to introduce herself as Liam's sister. Her features matched their mother's, although her hair was the color of a brown mouse and she didn't wear glasses.

"Liam. Oh my god, I didn't think we'd see you today after you didn't show at Dad's funeral." The greeting wasn't exactly friendly, although Charlotte caught a hint in her tone, as if his appearance at today's festivities was somehow a relief to her.

"Merry Christmas, Kara. Where's Bill today?"

Her eyes darted toward Mrs. Morris before settling back on him. "Working, unfortunately. The firm needed him on a case in Japan."

"Japan! Wow. So far away on a holiday. Too bad."

"It was unfortunate."

"Second year in a row," Mrs. Morris chimed in from across the room.

"I'm sure he'll make it next year, Mother," Kara protested, rolling her eyes. When they settled again, they perused her with a critical gaze. "And who is this?"

"This is my girlfriend, Charlotte," Liam said.

Kara offered a wide smile and shook her hand. "Wherever did he find you? Let me guess, lingerie model or actress?"

Although she held no judgment against either of those jobs, Charlotte didn't like Kara's dismissive tone, as if her following those career paths invalidated her as a person. Out of the corner of her eye, she saw Liam open his mouth to deliver a retort, but she beat him to the punch. "The North Pole," she said through a smile. "We worked together on a project."

Kara made a choking sound. "You're a scientist?"

She stood straighter. "There's nothing that interests me more than understanding this world."

"Well... uh... hmm." Kara tucked her hair behind her ear and joined Spencer and Mrs. Morris by the tree.

"Oh, gingerbread," Liam said, turning to a plate at

the end of the bar as if there had been nothing strange or unusual about that interaction. He handed her a brown cookie with white frosting.

She took it from him but didn't take a bite. "What is going on here, Liam?" she whispered. "Your family acts like they hate each other. They're so... unwelcoming."

Liam sighed. "I told you. This is what they're like. All part of the Christmas experience." He shoved a cookie in his mouth and chewed.

"No wonder you hate the holiday." Another servant in black and white asked what they'd like to drink, and she gestured toward Liam. "Surprise me."

Liam ordered her something called a Kentucky Buck. "Try the cookie."

She took a bite. "It's delicious. But *why* is everyone so angry? I thought you said she invited you. This can't all be about what happened with you?"

"Very little of it is about me actually," he mumbled. "I'm not entirely sure there is an explanation for how they are. Being rich and entitled asshats plays a big part."

"Mountain. I believed you when you told me about them, but it's so much more vivid in person."

He nodded. "We'll leave right after dinner, I promise."

The bartender slid a reddish cocktail into her hand. She took a sip, then followed Liam back into the living room.

Mrs. Morris snuffed her cigarette out in a ceramic ashtray. "I have to admit, when I asked you to come this year, I wasn't sure all of you would."

"Your call made it seem important," Liam said.

"It is important. The most important thing I've had to share with you in a long time."

Spencer and Kara drifted closer, the ice in their drinks rattling in their hands.

"As you all know, when your father died, he left the business and all his assets to me. He shared his wishes with me about what he wanted to happen with those assets. Roger didn't want a cent to go to Liam. He thought Spencer should get the lion's share as the one most involved with the company and Kara, as the corporation's attorney, should get the rest."

Charlotte couldn't miss how Kara crossed her arms and pouted at this news while Spencer smiled wide enough that she could see dollar signs in his pupils.

But Liam only sighed. "This is old news. I don't care about the money."

"You never did, did you?" Mrs. Morris said. "I guess that's proof enough that you're hers."

"Hers?" Kara drummed her fingers on her biceps. "What are you talking about?"

"This family has harbored a secret for decades, and it's time to let the skeleton out of the closet."

"Mom, please!" Liam held up a hand. But the universal sign for stop had no effect on Mrs. Morris.

"Your brother Liam isn't mine," Mrs. Morris said

casually. "He's the product of an affair between your father and a housekeeper who used to work here. Your father went to great lengths to keep this a secret, but I'm tired of secrets."

"Mom, this isn't the way to do this," Liam said.

"Wait, you knew about this?" Spencer glared at Liam.

Liam nodded. "For decades."

"Oh yes. We knew," Mrs. Morris said. "And it drove Roger crazy when Liam didn't want to be part of Morrismart, given where he'd come from. He always thought you should be more grateful, Liam, for the gift he gave you."

"Gift?"

"Being your father of course." She gave a low laugh.

"What's this about, Mom? Why are you bringing this up now?" Liam seemed incredibly annoyed by the turn of events, and Charlotte couldn't blame him. It seemed like a betrayal of his confidence to reveal it as she had.

"Because like I said, the money is mine now and Roger's wishes are buried with him. As it turns out, I will be soon as well."

"What?" Kara gasped. "Mother?"

"Cancer. Stage four. The doctors say I have six months."

"My god." Spencer reached for her, but she waved him away.

"Pull yourself together, Spencer."

Liam glanced at Charlotte before asking, "Was that the big announcement? You have cancer?"

His mother nodded slowly. "I want you all to know what my decision is concerning the money. My money. My business. My decision that will follow my death. Roger has no say anymore. It's mine."

Charlie moved closer to Liam, threading her fingers into his. She couldn't imagine what this must be like for him, learning he'd soon lose his mother after so recently losing his father and having her only focus be money he didn't even want.

"I've decided to split everything between the three of you evenly. Spencer will get the business and all its assets. Kara and Liam, you'll both get an equivalent amount once the rest of the estate is liquidized."

"Are you kidding me?" Kara said. "Liam hasn't been a part of this family for years! He's never been a part of the business."

Mrs. Morris held up a hand. "I'd like to change that, Kara. Liam, I want to name you a silent partner. You'll get the money and won't have to do a thing. You can spend it all on your little projects."

"But he'll just spend it on environmental initiatives that will only make things more difficult for Morrismart!" Spencer protested. Wild-eyed, he tossed back the remainder of his drink.

"He can spend it all on cat toys for all I care." Mrs. Morris reached into her jacket and pulled out another cigarette, then lit the tip. "All the paperwork has been executed with my lawyers and it's all airtight, so don't even think about challenging him over this, you understand? I'll write you out of the will so fast your head will spin."

Spencer and Kara glanced at each other, their lips curling with disdain. Liam was motionless.

"Are you okay?" Charlotte whispered.

He didn't answer, just stared straight ahead.

Mrs. Morris sucked in another lungful of smoke. "All right. That's it. That's the big announcement. Now, let's eat." She strode toward the hall, leaving them all gawking after her.

"Liam?" Charlie rubbed his back.

He raised a brow and then nodded slowly. "Yeah. Yeah, I'm okay."

NINETEEN

Liam shifted uncomfortably, realizing his brother and sister weren't going to say anything about what just happened. Someone needed to say something. "Mom, stop,"

She stopped and turned on those ridiculous heels of hers. What dying woman wore Louboutins?

"What is it, Liam? Don't tell me you don't want the money. I mean it when I say there are no strings attached."

He shook his head. "Shouldn't we talk about this? Isn't there anything we can try? Chemo? Radiation?" Jesus, why wasn't Spencer or Kara chiming in here?

She sighed. "Have you ever known me not to turn over every stone?"

"No." Liam crossed his arms and leaned back on his heels.

"So then take my word for it, boy. Now, I don't

want to spend my Christmas talking about cancer or money. Buck up or cry if you have to, and let's eat. Unless you'd like to share a smoke first?" She lifted her cigarette higher.

He shook his head.

"Yeah. Probably a good choice. You still need your lungs." She turned and strode toward the dining room.

That's when his siblings swarmed in.

"What the hell, Liam? How long has this been going on?" Spencer hissed.

"This what?" he asked defensively.

"Oh, come on. You must have been working on Mother behind our backs," Kara accused. "To have her turn on a dime like that? Well, don't think I'm not going to fight this."

He shook his head and scoffed. "I haven't talked to Mom since she called me to let me know Dad died, and that was a two-minute conversation. I'm as surprised as you."

Spence's eyes narrowed to slits. "Are you suggesting she did this on her own?"

Folding her arms over her chest, Kara rolled her eyes. "Of course not. I'm texting the firm. I want to see the paperwork."

"Aren't you two concerned at all that our last living parent is leaving us soon?" Liam asked.

They both looked at him and sighed.

"*Yes*," Kara said, exaggerating the word. "Of course

we care. But you heard her. She doesn't want us expressing it right now."

Spencer heaved a heavy sigh. "Listen to Kara, Liam. Don't ruin Christmas." He patted him on the shoulder twice, then turned and padded toward the dining room with Kara following.

"Jesus..." Liam wasn't sure what had gotten into his mother. But whether she felt guilty about the sins of the past or was changed by her approaching death, he wouldn't be rejecting this gift. There was a lot of good he could do in the world with that money. And although he thought he should feel sad and upset about her shuffling off this mortal coil, those feelings hadn't kicked in yet. Maybe he was in shock.

"Are you sure you're okay? This was... a lot," Charlotte said.

He nodded. "Yeah."

A fleeting thought coasted through his mind as he looked at her. This was a win for his relationship with Charlotte too. Now he could keep her in the lifestyle she was accustomed to. That is, if she decided to stay. And why wouldn't she now? He took her hand and led her into the dining room.

"Humans are so unpredictable," she whispered.

"Dragons too, at least by my experience." He cracked his neck, remembering Gabriel's grip.

She gave a breathy laugh. "In truth, that wasn't entirely unexpected. I mean, I didn't expect him back so early. That part was a surprise. But my father is a warrior with a short fuse and deep protective instincts for his mate and family. I mean, look what happened with Uncle Colin, and he's just my uncle."

"Sounds noble." He cracked his neck again.

"He'll come around," she said confidently, her eyes on his mother. "People change."

He scoffed.

"You don't think so?" She blinked up at him.

"You defied his orders. I doubt he's going to have warm fuzzy feelings about either of us after that." He pulled out her chair and tucked her in to the table, seating himself beside her. But the tears gathering in her eyes tugged at his heart. "But yeah, it's clear he loves you. I think, with time, he'll come around."

She flashed him a bright smile.

"What are you two whispering about down there?" his mother yelled from the head of the table. The thing could seat twenty, and the five of them were practically in different time zones. He picked up his fork and started picking at the pear-and-walnut salad that awaited them.

"Charlotte was just commenting on the beautiful table arrangement," he offered.

She hooked her pinky into his under the table.

"It's a family heirloom," his mom quipped.

Liam knew that of course. The terra-cotta cornucopia had been in their family for generations, all the way back to a great-great-great-grandmother who had found it in Athens.

"Charlotte hasn't heard the story, Mom," Spencer said, flashing his car-salesman smile.

"Oh, you've got to tell it. It's so creepy," Kara said with a shiver.

Charlotte smiled around a bite of salad. "I'd love to hear it."

"Oh, it's a fucking hoot," his mother said. "One of those tall tales that gets handed down over the years—you know the type. You've probably heard your share of them growing up in New Orleans. Don't they believe in witches, vampires, and voodoo down there?"

Charlotte swallowed her bite and gave a shallow laugh. "Among other things."

"Okay, then you'll find the humor in this." His mother set her fork down and toyed with the emeralds on her neck. "All the way back in 365 AD, there was an earthquake in Crete and a fissure opened up in the land behind my husband's ancestor's home. Her name was Iris Diamandis, which means diamonds, but it was a misnomer. She was an orphan and a pauper with no husband, who was barely surviving by selling herself on the street. Legend has it that when she went out to the fissure, she saw a blind man in it, perched precariously on a stony ledge inside the fiery chasm."

Charlotte's face paled, and she set down her fork. Liam squeezed her hand, but it had gone cold.

"Well, the man begged for her help and Iris complied immediately, casting a rope down and helping him out. As the story goes, he was so grateful that he gave her this cornucopia, which was his only possession. He told her that as long as she and her descendants kept it and displayed it prominently in their home, they and their relations would experience abundance like she could only imagine. Afterward, the man disappeared, but Iris took his words to heart and saved the cornucopia. The very next day, she bumped into a man while fetching water. He fell head over heels in love with her and married her that week. He was a wealthy dignitary from Rome and moved her into his palace. Since then, the cornucopia has passed down from generation to generation, and it has brought with it abundant wealth. As long as it remains in the possession of someone in her bloodline, so will the money. Roger believed all our success was thanks to this cornucopia." She laughed. "So we keep it in the china cabinet and pull it out every holiday. I suppose it fits in better at Thanksgiving, but the last thing I want to do is anger the god who gave it to her."

Beside him, Charlotte swallowed. "Is that the legend? That it was a *god* who gave it to her? I thought you said it was a blind man?"

"He was! At least that's the story. A blind Greek god, can you imagine? Don't ask me how he got stuck in the chasm! Doesn't seem very godlike to me."

"My guess is it was Plutus, the god of wealth," Charlotte said wistfully. "He was blinded by Zeus so that he couldn't discriminate to whom he gave his gifts. Before then, it is said, he only gave wealth to the good, but blinded, how could he tell who was good and who was evil? Only, in your Iris's case, he found a way. By saving him from the chasm, she proved her worthiness."

Everyone at the table stared at her. "You seem very knowledgeable about the subject," Kara said.

"She majored in Greek mythology," Liam blurted.

Spencer tucked in his chin. "I thought you said she was working with you at the North Pole?"

"She was. She, uh, was a double major of course. Greek mythology is a hobby of hers."

Beside him, Charlotte stiffened. It was an obvious lie. He could feel her retreating into herself. Maybe it was a bad idea bringing her here after all.

"I'll take care of the cornucopia after you're gone, Mother," Kara offered.

Liam smirked. Of course she would.

"No," his mother said flatly. They all looked toward the head of the table. His mother dabbed her mouth with a napkin and added, "It has to go to Liam."

"What? Mom!" Spencer looked absolutely beside himself.

Liam spread his hands. "Mom, I appreciate what you're trying to do here, but honestly, they can have it. I live in a tiny apartment. I don't even have a china cabinet."

His mom removed her glasses and pinched the bridge of her nose.

Beside him, Charlotte had gone deathly still, a grave look upon her face. "It has to be you, Liam," she said slowly. "This isn't about money—it's about blood."

His mother snorted. "It seems the blond bombshell is far smarter than she looks."

He ignored his mother's rude comment and glared at Charlotte, willing her to explain.

Charlotte gestured toward the cornucopia, her expression taking on an apologetic quality. "This is a magical object, Liam, and it requires Diamandis's blood to work. You are the only child with your father's blood."

He glanced between her and his mother. But she wasn't his mother, was she? Not really. His father had had an affair. But Spencer and Kara were also his children, weren't they?

Charlotte squeezed his hand. He'd never stopped to consider that perhaps his father wasn't the only one to have an affair. He looked at his brother; his mother's sharp nose and blue eyes stared back at him. Kara's features were similar. Only he had his father's brown eyes and aquiline nose.

His mother replaced her glasses. "They're not his, Liam. The future of the Morris fortune relies on you now."

TWENTY

Charlie's skin felt too tight, and it wasn't just because her wings were magically crammed inside her and it was starting to become uncomfortable. Or that she was starving and if she didn't eat something soon, she'd be too weak to maintain her illusion. That cornucopia was a gift of the gods. She could feel the celestial magic buzzing against her skin, calling her true nature out of her. The tension in the room among these humans added to the uncomfortable prickle. She shifted in her seat.

"That's why you're giving me the money." Liam leaned back in his chair, adding a grunt of disgust for good measure. "Dad didn't know, and if I don't take the cornucopia, you're afraid you'll lose it all."

Mrs. Morris bared her teeth. "I'm not afraid of anything, son. I won't be here to see the worst of it, and I assure you my last days on this earth have already been taken care of."

"Everyone needs to stop," Spencer said. "It's not true! I demand a paternity test!"

His mother rolled her eyes. "I was there when you were conceived, Spencer. Trust me on this one."

Liam's head listed to the side. "Jesus. This can't be happening."

Kara huffed. "I knew it. I never felt any connection to Dad. He was always so distant."

Liam scoffed. "He wasn't any closer to his blood, sweetheart."

A horrified look cast over Spencer's face, and he stared at the cornucopia. "You don't think that's why...?"

"Morrismart stock has tumbled since your father's passing?" Mrs. Morris took out another cigarette and lit up. "I can find no other reason."

At that moment, a team of servants entered the room, swept away their mostly uneaten salads, and replaced them with a whole creature with a shell and claws that stared back at Charlotte with beady black eyes.

"What is this?" she asked Liam under her breath.

"Lobster thermidor. You just eat the tail part."

Spencer, who must have read their lips from across the table, shook his head and spread his hands. "Who the hell is this chick? An environmental scientist with a side of Greek mythology who has never seen a lobster before?" He stood up and threw his napkin onto the table. "You know what I think? I think that slut is a corporate raider who's been working with Liam to undercut Morrismart's stock price and convince a dying woman that some family story about a piece of pottery is true."

Kara raised a finger. "That makes sense. Liam has probably known about us all along. He said he knew about Dad's affair."

"God, Liam, how low can you go? Convincing our dying mother that all this cornucopia nonsense is real just so you can get your hands on Dad's money?" Spencer sneered at him.

Liam shook his head. "That's bullshit, Spence. I didn't have anything to do with this."

Mrs. Morris gave a gritty laugh and drew another puff on her cigarette. "You idiots couldn't tell the truth from your own ass in a mirror. Liam didn't know a thing about this. And you can doubt the family folklore... God knows I did until that bastard left me behind, but it's true, and that man"—she pointed at Liam—"is your only hope of maintaining the lifestyle you're accustomed to. If he takes the money and the cornucopia, you stay in business."

Pain ricocheted through her body, and Charlotte had to close her eyes to keep from spreading her wings. Out of desperation, she shoved a large bite of lobster into her mouth and chewed. Liam stared at her as she shoveled in another bite and washed it down with the white wine in front of her.

"Charlotte?" he asked softly.

"I need to get out of here," she said, taking another bite. She gave him a loaded look, trying to project into his head how important it was that she eat. "I'm *really* hungry, Liam, and I'm afraid something bad will happen if I don't eat."

"Okay, I uh…" He stood and turned toward his family. "Charlotte and I have to go. She's not feeling well."

Kara lurched to her feet. "Bullshit. You're staying. We're figuring this out."

Liam looked to Charlotte. She closed her eyes and said, "It's real, Liam. All of it. Everything your mother said. If you touch it, you'll know."

Spencer tossed up his hands. "Jesus Christ. Now we're listening to mystery slut over having a logical conversation about this?"

Liam was around the table in a heartbeat, his hand clutching Spencer's throat until he made a gagging sound. "You call my girl a name again and I'll shove your face into the truth. And by the truth, I mean your ass. I just said truth since Mom's right—you can't tell the difference between the two." He shoved him back into his chair and then turned to face the cornucopia.

Charlotte folded her hands and waited. His blood was the key to this gift of the gods, and the moment he touched it, he'd feel the truth in it. With one more glance toward his mom, Liam leaned over the side of the table and placed his hand on the terra-cotta. Light flowed from the gift, up his arm, turning Liam's brown eyes golden.

Kara blocked the light with a raised arm, her mouth dropping open. All the blood had drained from Spencer's face. Mrs. Morris was laughing and shaking her head like the entire experience was delightful. Charlie couldn't figure her out. She'd announced she was dying, pitted her children against each other, and now was experiencing something that had to challenge her human perceptions. And yet she looked... happy. Wickedly happy. As if she was hiding some dark secret.

An uneasy feeling overcame her as Liam pulled away his hand. She stood from her chair. "We should go."

Liam's face was blank. He was staring at his hands is if he'd only recently discovered they were attached to his body.

"I knew it was true," Mrs. Morris said. "And now everything is going to be okay."

"Everything..." A chill traveled through Charlotte as she watched the woman inhale hard on her cigarette.

"A deal is a deal." She winked. "Take it from me, chicky, the art of the deal doesn't end with this life."

"What did you do?" Charlie glanced toward Liam

as a pinprick of light sparked against the wall behind his mother.

"What the fuck is that?" Spencer knocked over his chair getting up and stumbled backward toward the window.

"Liam! Come to me." Charlie held out her hand. She could protect him. She could jump with him to another dimension if she had to.

The golden glow spread into a human shape, but that was no human. Her only question was, which one. Which god had Mrs. Morris made a deal with and why?

The light gathered until winged shoes and a helmet came into view. "Hermes."

The messenger god formed beside Mrs. Morris and dropped a coin onto the table in front of her, a Greek obol. "Your passage to Elysium, courtesy of Plutus."

She snatched the coin from the table and gripped it in her palm.

"What did you trade for the obol?" Charlie asked, pinning her with a stare.

She shook her head. "Nothing more than helping Plutus continue what he started, girl. He was blinded to keep him from discriminating. He *wants* to discriminate. Liam's existence and acceptance of the gift means he gets what he wants for another generation. Everyone is happy."

Kara thrust her hand into her purse and pulled out a gun, pointing it at Liam. "Not everyone."

Liam raised his hands. "Kara... Come on..."

"Put it down, you fool. If he dies, you lose everything," Mrs. Morris said.

She shook her head. "I don't think so. I think if he dies, we lose the magic but we keep the money. All of it."

Her gaze connected to Spencer's.

Charlie observed all that in her peripheral vision as her attention was locked on Hermes, who hadn't left the room. He was studying her and smiling in that unreadable way of the gods. And he was waiting. Waiting for her to confirm what he already suspected, what he could likely feel across the room just as she could feel him.

Her stomach cramped with the need to spread her wings.

She'd never taken her parents' warnings about the danger of leaving Paragon too seriously. As far as she was aware, the gods were too wrapped up in themselves to have much interest in people's everyday lives. Certainly, her small life wouldn't attract much attention, or so she'd assumed. But here was proof that she was wrong about that.

"Do it!" Spencer yelled.

"Don't be stupid, Kara!" Mrs. Morris yelled. "Look at me. Look at me!"

Charlie's power snapped to attention as Kara's breath left her lungs. She blinked once, and then her finger twitched, discharging the gun. Liam threw himself out of the way, but he wasn't fast enough.

Crossing her arms, Charlotte extended her shield, catching the bullet before it could burrow into Liam's neck. But the celestial magic it cost Charlie came at a price. Her wings unfurled with a snap. She grunted with the effort, panting and staggering. The bullet dropped harmlessly onto the table, but she was drained. Liam caught her around the waist.

"Guardian, who sent you?" Hermes boomed, his head cocking to the side.

"Guardian?" Mrs. Morris scowled. "What are you talking about? What is she, Liam? What have you done?"

"You are mistaken, Lord Hermes." Charlie said. "I am no guardian. I am a demigod, descended of Circe."

His laugh rippled in the room around them. "Of course you are, *princess of Paragon*. What a pleasure it is to finally make your acquaintance." He bowed. "Although you must know that Olympus will have to be informed of your visit to this realm."

"Why?"

He took a step toward her, his feet never touching the ground as the wings on his sandals fluttered. Hermes was not a warrior god, only a messenger. He would not harm her, but he wasn't harmless. As he reached out a hand to her and flashed his most seductive smile, she knew he was trying to lure her in.

Other, far more dangerous, gods would reward him handsomely if he succeeded.

"Only to introduce you to your kind," he said smoothly. "You are one of us, Princess. Why are you wasting yourself among humans? Olympus will want to welcome you properly."

Liam stepped in front of her. "Go, Charlotte," he whispered to her over his shoulder.

She took a step back, her legs shaking. "I'm not strong enough to carry us both."

"Go without me. Please. Now!"

Hermes's smile morphed into something far more sinister, his lips pulling back from his teeth. Blinding light filled the room.

Liam covered his eyes with his arm, screaming, "Go, Charlotte, go!"

Charlie had no choice but to do as he said. She was too weak for anything else. She pivoted, sliced open a portal between dimensions, and traveled home.

TWENTY-ONE

Charlie slammed into the stone floor of her ritual room, facedown and covered in sweat, trembling uncontrollably. Tears spilled from her eyes, her body wracked with sobs. She covered her face with her hands, curling onto her side. Oh gods, what had she done? She'd left Liam to Hermes's mercy.

Strong arms gathered her up. She gasped and blinked in surprise at her father's scent.

"I've got you, sweetheart. I've got you."

As angry as she was at him, it felt good. He loved her. No matter what, she knew that to be true. Maybe that was why she'd returned herself to the same hour she left. Although she'd been gone for days, to her father, she'd been gone maybe forty minutes or so. He'd obviously been waiting for her return.

She sobbed harder. Why was she such a coward? She'd left Liam in an impossible situation. She should have stayed. She should have faced Hermes and protected Liam. What would happen now?

Her father set her on her bed and brushed her hair back from her face. "What happened? Do you want to talk about it?"

"I have to go back," she croaked. She pushed herself to a seated position and wiped under her eyes, blinking rapidly.

Gabriel folded himself into the chair next to her bed, his face somber. "Where did you get that dress?"

She froze. Purple sequins were not a thing in Paragon, and the cut was entirely human. "Macy's," she said simply.

Her father swallowed and gripped the arms of his chair. "How long were you gone?"

"You tell me," she said softly.

"In your sequence of events, not in mine."

"Four days." She shivered, too exhausted to defend herself from his anger or to dodge his questions.

He leaned back in the chair and stared at the ceiling. "Thank you for coming back."

She hesitated, knowing that the truth could get her into a world of trouble but not caring anymore. Whatever punishment her father doled out, it couldn't be worse than the pain gripping her heart. What was happening to Liam? "I wanted to stay."

His brows ratcheted up and talons sprouted from his knuckles, digging into the arms of her chair.

"You're going to pull the stuffing out." She sniffed and pointed to the chair arms.

He lifted his claws, his throat bobbing before he gritted out, "Why did you want to stay?"

She sighed and wiped her eyes again, but there was no slowing the tears. "I love him, Dad. From the moment I saw him." Her breath caught. "Even in the beginning when I thought he was a miserable, gruff pain in the ass, I loved him. He made me feel alive. He made me feel like the world had color, and the thought of continuing on without him feels..."

"Gray?" he finished for her.

She nodded, and for the first time she saw sympathy in his eyes.

"I'm afraid you may have found a potential mate, Charlie. I wasn't sure it would work the same for you, not being entirely dragon, but what you're describing is how a felt about your mother. From the very beginning."

A sob broke from her throat, and she wept bitterly.

"Does he not feel the same way about you?"

She stared at her hands, remembering how Liam had placed his body between her and Hermes. He'd never told her he loved her, but he'd shown her. "He does. He'd die for me. I know he would."

Now her father looked truly puzzled. "Then why did you return without him? I was angry. I shouldn't have been so harsh with you. But I would have come around if—"

"I didn't leave him because of you."

He lowered his chin and narrowed his eyes. "Then why?"

"Hermes."

Now a growl rumbled from his chest and his talons punctured the fabric. "Did he touch you? How did you escape?"

"He tried. Liam's family has a history with the gods." She shook her head and then told him about the cornucopia, his father, and the strained relationship he shared with his family. "The coincidence of it all. How many humans are in that position? How am I so unlucky to fall in love with the one person from Earth I can't go to without putting myself in danger?"

Her father went perfectly still and deadly quiet, which she recognized as a far more dangerous state than when he was visibly angry. "I don't believe in coincidences, Charlie."

"But what else could it be but a coincidence?" She laughed skeptically. "I picked him up at the North Pole, for Mountain's sake!"

"What gave you the idea to go to the North Pole?"

"Aunt Avery was sad she'd miss Christmas, so I got the idea to throw her one, for when she came back here. I was looking at a book in the library and came across an entry about Christmas and Santa Claus. I decided to bring him here to help me."

Gabriel rubbed his head. "Show me the book."

Together they strode toward the library and to the

place where she'd returned the book. The gold cover reflected the light from the windows, and a warm feeling came over her as she removed it from the shelf.

"Hmmm."

"What?"

"Did your mom teach you a spell to identify traces of magic on an item?"

"Of course. I was doing that magic by the time I was twelve."

"Do it now."

"I need something from my stores." She hoisted the tome into her arms and carried it back into her chambers and into her ritual room where she selected a diamond from one of her bins and tied it to a string. Placing the book in the center of her symbol, she allowed the gem to circle over the cover while she muttered the spell she knew by heart, sending her intention and her power into the stone.

Three times around it went until the gem glowed golden like a star.

"Celestial magic," she confirmed.

Gabriel shook his head. "You meeting Liam was no coincidence, honey. One of the gods baited you. They wanted you off Ouros so they could reach you."

She tossed the stone aside and placed her hand on the cover, thrusting her power into the book. Celestial magic knew celestial magic. She sifted the deity's signature through a sieve of her magic. A few breaths later, she could barely keep her eyes open, but she had her answer. It tasted like sulfur.

"Hades."

"Hmmm. What would Hades want with you?" Gabriel asked.

She looked up at him. "I'm the one who got away, and I freed two souls when I did."

He nodded. "I think we have our answer."

"But how did he get this into our library?"

Gabriel frowned and reached for the book, referring to the details scribed in the front of the tome. "It's been here since my mother was regent. I'm guessing it was a gift from Hades with strings attached. After you escaped the fire dimension, he decided to pull the string."

Gods, she was tired, but this couldn't wait. "Stand back," she said, moving to her shelf and grabbing the stone vessel of the goddess's tears she'd had Leena bring her from Rogos. It was useful in scrying the future but also strong enough to destroy almost anything. She dribbled it carefully over the golden book and watched it melt into a pool of molten metal before evaporating into a puff of foul-smelling smoke.

After a moment of silence, her father reached over and grabbed her hand. "Just because he was your bait doesn't mean the feelings you felt for each other weren't real."

"Do you think Hermes or one of the others will try to use him to get to me?"

"Maybe."

She closed her eyes. "I could time jump back and take him with me, but I'm too tired and weak."

"Then eat and sleep," he said. "Time will still be there when you wake up."

She nodded. "Yeah, it will be. But he has a life there, Dad. It's one thing for me to follow him to Earth. I'm practically useless here."

"That's not true."

She shook her head. "You don't need me."

"You're wrong about that."

"I wouldn't blame him if he wanted to end it once he knew how he was used."

"You'd tell him?"

"I'd have to."

"I thought you said he was willing to die for you."

"He was."

"Then trust in that. No spell can fake love, Charlie. Not real love." He helped her to her feet, and they returned the tears to her shelf before heading for her room. "Lie down. I'll order you up some food."

"I thought you had to get back to Mom?"

"Let me worry about that. I'll send a falcon." He tucked her in and kissed her on the forehead. "Close your eyes. I'll have Rachel wake you up when she delivers your meal."

Her lids blinked shut, exhaustion drawing her under. "I love you, Dad."

"I love you too, Charlie, a hell of a lot more than I

love being right or than I love the traditions of this kingdom. I'm sorry I forgot that for a second."

And that was what she loved about her father. He was strong, firm handed, and forever the warrior, but he didn't hold back his emotions or his apologies when it mattered. Another wave of tears came over her. She was so hungry and tired. But under his watchful eyes, she drifted to sleep.

TWENTY-TWO

The light coming off Hermes wasn't just bright, it burned, and Liam kept his arms crossed over his eyes against it. What else could he do? He wasn't packing heat like Kara, and even if he was, what weapon would work against a god?

At least he knew Charlotte would be okay. She'd jumped, leaving him in a whoosh of feathers and a brush of startled air. He tried to feel good about that, but her absence was soul crushing. She wouldn't be back. She couldn't. Not now that the gods were waiting for her and watching him.

Gradually the light faded, Hermes reducing to the same pinprick of light he'd arrived as. "I will deliver the message," his voice boomed. Then he was gone.

"Fuck! Did you see that?" Spencer dug his fingers into his remaining hair. "Tell me you saw that! The wings and the glowing. The coin. Mom, what was with the coin?"

"It all happened, Spencer. Now shut the fuck up." Kara was staring at their mother like she wanted to kill her. At least she wasn't holding the gun anymore. It lay on the table beside her purse.

"You tried to shoot me," Liam said to Kara, his eyes on the gun.

"So?" She stared at him impassively, as if the idea still seemed like a good one to her. Fuck, he'd thought she was distant and aloof before. Not exactly sisterly, but now he realized she was a sociopath.

"After what happened today, Liam, I think we can all agree the situation got out of hand. Let's just move beyond it," Spencer said.

"Move beyond it? You told Kara to shoot me."

"I was triggered!" He spread his hands. "The way Mom sprang all that stuff on us. You understand, right?"

Liam stared at his mother, her fist still clenched around the coin. "You've been planning this for some time, haven't you?"

His mother snorted. "Since your father died and he told me on his deathbed that it was all true. He laughed, you know. Thought he was really sticking it to me. We hated each other by the end."

Liam looked from his sister to his brother to his mother and felt no attachment whatsoever. These people didn't care if he lived or died. This was all about them. By giving him a share of the business, she was tying his wealth to theirs. By giving him the cornucopia, she was ensuring their wealth continued indefinitely, and by doing both things in service to Plutus, she ensured her place in the underworld. No one in this room cared about what he did. They didn't care if he lived or died or saved the planet just as long as he took that ugly-ass centerpiece with him.

And his siblings were willing to kill him over the difference between being billionaires and being marginally wealthier billionaires. Their greed was astounding. He never wanted to have a reason to be in the same room with them again.

The money would be nice.

He could do plenty of good with it.

And he'd never be able to live with himself if he took it.

"I don't want it," he said.

"Don't want what?" his mother asked.

"I don't want the money, the silent partnership, or the cornucopia. I reject it all. You are not my family."

The air shimmered with his decision, a pulse coming from the ancient gift at the center of the table. He headed for the door.

"No, no, no!" his mother screamed. "The coin. Liam, the coin is gone! Come back please. I beg you. LIAM!"

He accepted his coat from the butler.

"You'll regret this," his mother cried from the

dining room. "I will ruin you! I will destroy everything you love!"

"You already did," he muttered, the crushing truth that Charlotte was really gone settling over him.

BACK IN HIS TINY LAKE VIEW APARTMENT FOUR DAYS LATER, Liam bit into one of the chocolate chip cookies Charlotte and he had made and tried to hold himself together. He'd been saving them like some kind of shrine to her, but they were going to go stale soon, and the last thing he wanted was to throw them away. They tasted good but turned to ash in his mouth as he thought about Charlotte. Why had he taken her to meet his family? He should have played it safe, hidden her here for as long as he could have gotten away with it.

God, he missed her. Even burying himself in his work hadn't helped this time. He couldn't stop thinking about her.

He grabbed the bottle of bourbon from the top of the fridge and poured himself a glass, washing down the cookie with a healthy swig. He wasn't sure how he was going to survive this world without her, now truly alone as he was, but he guessed there would be a lot of bourbon involved.

A knock came on the door. Probably Mrs. Thornton with his mail again. You'd think the damned post office would learn to read an address. But when he unlocked the door, death was waiting for him on the other side. He tried to close it again, but the man's hand shot out and held it open.

"Hello, Liam," Charlotte's father said.

Liam raised both hands in front of him. "She's not here. Mr. Uh...?"

"Gabriel. Call me Gabriel."

"Gabriel."

"I know she's not here. I just left her in Paragon. In that timeline, she's just returned from Christmas with your family."

"Oh. That was a few days ago."

"Can we speak?"

He nodded and backed up, letting him in. Fuck, the guy was big. Professional-wrestler big. If this got ugly, Liam would definitely end up on the losing end. He closed the door.

"Drink?"

"What've you got?"

"Bourbon. Wine. I might have a beer in the back of the fridge."

"Bourbon is fine."

Liam poured him a glass while the guy took a seat on his sofa, seeming to take up the entire thing. He handed him his glass and then perched on the chair across the coffee table from him.

"Is she okay?"

Gabriel frowned. "It depends on your definition of

okay. She's not physically harmed. But she was... devastated to have to leave you behind. Worried about what Hermes might do to you."

"Honestly, I was too. I'm still worried. Hermes said he was going to tell the other gods what happened. No one's come for me yet, but I know it's possible. It doesn't matter though. The only thing I was concerned about was getting Charlotte out of there. I'm relieved she's safe."

Gabriel swirled the ice in his glass. Took a deep drink. "My guess is they're watching you. Using you as bait. They're hoping she comes back for you."

"You've got to make sure that doesn't happen," Liam said quickly. The last thing he wanted was to be the reason they captured her. "She can't risk herself for me. I won't allow it."

"You love her?"

Liam swallowed hard, glancing down at the drink in his hands. This wasn't supposed to be the way this happened. Her father wasn't supposed to be the first one to know, not before he even had a chance to tell her. But then, her safety was the priority, which meant he might never have a chance to tell her anyway.

"More than anything. I love her in a way I never thought possible." He drained his glass. "Which is why you've got to do whatever it takes to keep her from coming here. If she does, I won't be able to send her away. I can't deny her anything she asks for, you know?"

Gabriel rubbed his jaw and laughed. "Yeah, I know."

God, he hated this. It felt as though his soul was being torn out of his body to have this connection to her but know it was temporary. Know it was his final goodbye.

In the silence that followed, Gabriel looked around the tiny apartment, growing visibly perplexed. "Now that you have the cornucopia, I imagine you'll be... upgrading soon."

Liam shook his head. "I rejected it. Left it with my... The family I grew up with."

"You rejected it?" Now Gabriel's expression was almost angry with confusion.

"It would have bound me to them, and they are evil people, Gabriel. Truly evil. I could have done good things with the money, but they'd have canceled out everything I did with their own actions. Besides, having that would only attract the attention of the gods, and that's the last thing I want."

"You were hoping if you left it behind, you'd leave them behind... in case she came back."

He frowned. "Maybe, in the moment."

"But now you know that's not possible, right? If she comes here, they'll know. They'll be waiting."

He nodded. It was all he could do with his throat as tight as it was. He took another drink, thankful for the numbing effects of the alcohol, then cleared his throat. "So if you came here to kill me or something, I don't think you need to. I'd never hurt her. I love her. And as it is, it looks like fate will keep us apart anyway."

"That's the thing, Liam. I know my daughter. I know her heart. And I don't think she'll stay away from you. She loves you too much."

He closed his eyes against the painful squeeze that caused in his chest. "What do you want me to do?"

"I think you've got to make this right. I think you're the only one who can."

What did he want from him? He'd already told him he wasn't strong enough to push her away if she did come. "How exactly am I supposed to do that from here?"

"You can't." Gabriel set his glass on the side table and stood up, looming over him like a dark cloud. "The only way to make this right is for you to come back to Paragon with me."

He snorted. "What? To tell her goodbye? To push her away?" He shook his head. He couldn't do it.

"No," Gabriel said. "To marry her."

TWENTY-THREE

Had Liam heard him correctly? Marry her. "You'd allow your daughter to marry a human?"

Gabriel snorted, then broke into a laugh that seemed uncharacteristically robust. "I'm married to a human."

"A witch."

"Are you refusing my offer?" Gabriel asked, all levity leaving his features. "Perhaps your work here—"

"No," Liam said quickly, all his former passion for his work and his place on this planet paling against the desire to see Charlotte again. "I want to go with you. I very much want to marry Charlotte."

"Good."

"Only—"

"Only...?"

"She gets a choice. I will ask her. I will leave this

life and happily marry her. But I won't force her. If she says no, you bring me back here."

Gabriel seemed almost amused by this declaration. "Deal. Let's go."

Liam stood, eyes darting around his tiny abode. "Wait, should I pack a bag or something?"

"Only if there's something you can't live without. Everything you need, I'll make sure is provided for you."

"I don't have a ring to offer her."

Gabriel's smile grew wider. "I can help you with that as well."

Liam dropped his hands to his sides, taking one last look at the apartment he'd called home for almost six years. Now it was just a room, one whose importance didn't hold a candle to the woman he hoped was in his future. "I'm ready."

CHARLOTTE WOKE CRYING. AFTER A MEAL SHE'D HARDLY tasted, she'd fallen back to sleep and dreamed of being with Liam. She'd felt his hand in hers, heard that rare laugh that seemed to only come out for her, smelled his distinct scent. And then she woke up and it was all gone. All she had was her room in Paragon and memories of their time together.

Footsteps outside her room drew her attention. Heavy footsteps. Probably her father. Now that she'd rested, he'd want to return to Darnuith. As a dragon, his every instinct was to protect her mother. She could only imagine how hard it must be for him to be away from her now. As destroyed as she felt on the inside, she'd pull herself together for his sake.

"Charlotte."

Her breath caught in her throat. That was Liam's voice. Was she hallucinating? She was almost afraid to look in the direction of the sound. Afraid to find someone else there or no one at all. But she couldn't help herself.

And he *was* there. Dressed in dark jeans and a Blackhawks jersey, he looked as if he'd stepped off the streets of Chicago and arrived in her bedroom. She didn't miss the stubble on his chin or the dark circles under his eyes though. By the look of things, Liam had struggled with their separation as much as she had.

"Liam? What are you doing here?" She sat up in bed, wiping under her swollen eyes. She didn't need a mirror to know her face was red and puffy and her hair was probably a rat's nest. But she didn't care. All she cared about was the man in front of her. If this wasn't real, if she was dreaming, she never wanted to wake up.

He moved closer to her. "Your dad came to get me," he said softly.

"He did?" Her gaze drifted to his throat. No finger marks. That was a good sign.

"We, uh, made our peace. Actually, he's a pretty cool guy... Um, dragon."

Her heart warmed as she realized what her father had done. But what was his purpose? Had he brought Liam here so that she'd know he was safe? Or so they could say goodbye?

"I'm so glad you're okay. I was worried Hermes might hurt you or try to use you to get to me."

He shook his head. "I'm fine. Well, I will be once we have a chance to talk." He came to stand in front of her. "Charlotte, I've been thinking about the day you came to get me. You appeared on that sheet of ice, glowing like a star, and I wondered if I'd died." He laughed and glanced down at his hands. "I thought you were there to take me to heaven."

She gave a breathy laugh. "Sorry. I didn't mean to scare you, but in my defense, I thought you were someone else."

He reached out and brushed her hair back from her face. "The thing is, I was right."

"Huh?"

"I did die that day, in a way." He rubbed the back of his neck. "I'd spent so many years studying science and thinking I knew exactly how the universe worked. The only things I believed in were the things I could experience through my senses. I had no faith. I had no real family. All I had was my work, and as important as that work was, there was no joy in it for me anymore.

It was only a distraction from the things I didn't want to face or feel."

"After meeting your family, it's pretty clear to me how you got there, Liam."

He held up a hand. "But then you came, and everything I thought I knew was challenged in an instant. And you, you didn't just glow. You were a light to me. You were my light, guiding me to shore. I don't know when it happened exactly, but knowing you, coming here, it reconnected me to who I was, to the joy I thought had been drained out of my existence years ago."

"It's still there. I love to hear you laugh."

He cupped her chin in his hand, searching her eyes. "I love you, Charlotte."

A swarm of butterflies took flight within her, and she couldn't stop the smile that took over her expression. "I love you too. So much."

"Your father brought me back here because I don't want to be apart from you anymore." He reached into his pocket and pulled out a ring. She gasped at the beautiful piece. It was gold, an intricately designed star shape. The metal was decorated with a radiant blue diamond at its center. "Full disclosure—Gabriel helped me with this one. I'm afraid blue diamonds are not within the budget of an academic."

"It's gorgeous, Liam, but—"

"Charlotte, will you marry me?"

She gazed up at him, her every instinct simply to

yell yes and throw her arms around his neck, but she couldn't. Not without knowing for sure that this is what he wanted.

"You said my father came to see you. Did he... did he *encourage* you to do this?"

Liam laughed and shook his head. "No, Charlotte. He suggested it was a possibility, but I wanted this. Your dad did give me his blessing and help me with the ring though."

"But... I mean, you love what you do. Do you understand I can't leave here? Not without putting myself in danger. If we were married, you'd have to stay here... unless you're thinking we'd live apart."

"Hell no." He shook his head. "I don't want to live apart. This proposal comes with the understanding that I will stay here, not because I have to but because I want to. But there is one thing that can get me to go, and that's you sending me away. You can say no. I won't be angry, and you won't be putting me in danger. I only want you to say what's in your heart."

She reached out and took his hands in hers, new tears flowing down her cheeks. "My heart wanted me to say yes the second I saw you standing beside my bed." She slid her finger into the ring, admiring the rare purplish blue of the diamond. "Yes, Liam. I will marry you."

Taking her face in his hands, he wiped under her eyes with his thumbs, then met her mouth with his. A hum started in her veins, the same current of desire she'd felt the day she met him, but also something more. A connection. A recognition of him by her celestial blood that she'd found her other, her mate if dragon terms could be applied to her, and she'd never be alone again.

TWENTY-FOUR

Two weeks later, Charlotte waited in front of the massive Christmas tree in the great hall for her mom and aunts to return from Darnuith. They'd sent a falcon letting her know of their impending arrival and that the spell was a success. After the Darnuith witches reinstated the three sisters' magic, Avery had displayed accelerated healing powers and Nathaniel's magical tests had proven what Queen Penelope and the witches of Darnuith had suspected—her body had incorporated the tooth. She was, as far as anyone could tell, immortal.

"How's this look?" Liam yelled from the rafters where he'd hung a bit of greenery that was supposed to look like mistletoe.

"Perfect," she said. "Come down here and we'll put it to the test."

He climbed down the ladder, his tunic and boots

making him appear more like a dragon than a human. Leaping off the last rung and landing in front of her, he grabbed her waist and spun her under the mistletoe, dipping her back before kissing her soundly on the lips. He was still kissing her when voices startled them. He stood her up, laughing as he straightened her dress and his tunic.

"Oh my god, it's Christmas!" Avery squealed. She ran into the room, staring up at the tree and clasping her hands in front of her chest.

"Wow! It's a really good representation. This could be from Earth," Clarissa said, coming in behind her.

Her mother came in next, stared up at the tree, and then looked directly at her. "Charlotte, did you do this?"

Charlotte. She couldn't remember the last time her mother had called her by her full first name. "Yes. Aunt Avery said she was disappointed she was going to miss Christmas. So I threw a Christmas." She waved a hand toward the buffet of Christmas treats set up near the back of the room—cakes, cookies, and pastries in the shapes of trees and angels. Above her, lighted greenery twinkled beside the gorgeous tree, and the gifts she'd purchased for all of them sat in shiny wrappings underneath.

"It's incredible!" Avery said.

"Aye, 'tis!" Xavier added, wrapping his arms around his mate's shoulders.

Her father and Nathaniel entered the hall soon

after, both beaming when they saw the room. She bounced on her toes, even prouder than she'd expected to be at the joy she saw on all their faces.

Liam leaned close until his lips brushed her ear. "You did it. It's perfect, Charlotte."

She turned to him, blushing again. "We did it."

Raven strode toward them, her smile sparkling as bright as the tiara nestled in her dark hair. Without a word, she grabbed Charlotte by the shoulders and pulled her into a warm embrace. "You're incredible, you know that?"

She glanced toward her toes. "I'm so glad you like it."

Her mother dropped her hands and folded them behind her back, straightening and taking on the air of the queen she was. "I think the thing I find most impressive is that you did this while also leading the kingdom."

Charlotte raised her gaze to meet her mom's.

"Several Elder Council representatives confirmed that your leadership at the last meeting was inspired. They insist you lead in the future, and Marius agrees. He told me you were invaluable."

She nodded. "Thank you. I feel the meeting went well."

"I'm glad you think so because it's yours now. Marius has his hands full with other things, and Gabriel and I think it's time you took on more responsibility."

She beamed, nodding vigorously. "Of course. Yes. Thank you!"

She was still gushing when Raven's gaze shifted to Liam. "On another note, my mate tells me that you have some news."

Liam gave an awkward bow. "I'm Liam. It's an honor to finally meet you."

She inclined her head, then gave him a knowing smile. "And who are you to me, Liam?"

He cleared his throat, glanced at Charlotte, then said, "I'm your future son-in-law."

Charlotte giggled excitedly and held out her hand to her mother, showing off the ring.

Raven shook her head, her lips curling as if the entire thing amazed and delighted her. "I leave you for three weeks, Charlotte, and not only do you rise to the occasion for the kingdom, you throw a major party and find yourself a mate. If I haven't made it clearly obvious, you amaze me."

Gabriel swaggered up behind her and placed a hand on the queen's shoulder. "I agree. But let's not get ahead of ourselves. There's still a royal wedding to plan, and Liam has to be introduced to the kingdom. Not necessarily in that order."

Liam wrapped an arm around Charlotte's waist and pulled her into his side. "I'm ready."

"That's good, because there's plenty of work to do around this kingdom," Gabriel said. "And you've signed up for an extremely important role."

"Husband to your daughter?"

Gabriel smirked. "Prince of Paragon."

Liam gulped as her mother and father turned back toward the tree. "Is that true? Will I be...?"

"A prince? Yes, I'm afraid so."

He took a deep breath. "Okay. I'm sure I can learn."

"You'll do fine."

"So what's a royal wedding in Paragon like anyway?" Liam asked.

She shrugged. "Pretty much the same as a human wedding, I think, only bigger, and the entire kingdom will be watching. Oh, and they'll probably crown you as part of the ceremony."

He chewed his lip. "Can't be any harder than sampling ice in the middle of winter from the North Pole under the cover of darkness."

"Or delivering gifts to children around the world," she said with a half smile.

He shrugged. "Hey, you've made a believer out of me. Maybe there's something to be said for the legend of Santa Claus anyway."

"Oh?"

He pulled her close. "I, for one, got exactly what I wanted for Christmas."

She pressed her lips to his. "Me too. For this Christmas and every Christmas... Always."

❄

Thank you for reading the Angel of Paragon! Want a little more Charlie and Liam?
Click HERE for a bonus epilogue.

https://geni.us/angelbonusepilogue

In the TREASURE OF PARAGON, the witch queen of Darnuith is a legend and her true story is lost to history. Learn the truth behind the folklore in The Three Sisters Trilogy. Book 1, THE TANGLEWOOD WITCHES is available now! Get your copy, or continue on to read an excerpt

DON'T MISS THE TANGLEWOOD WITCHES

Flip the page to read an excerpt of the action-packed prequel to the TREASURE OF PARAGON, THE TANGLEWOOD WITCHES!

THE TANGLEWOOD WITCHES

Alexandria, Egypt, 30 BC

"Unhand me. I demand to know what this is about!" Alena grunted as the guard's palm rudely connected with the center of her back and thrust her into the stone cell with no regard for her ongoing protests.

This morning had gone from bad to worse. At the crack of dawn, a team of Egyptian soldiers had hauled her out of her meager lodgings and dragged her to Cleopatra's palace. The soldiers had offered no explanation for her arrest. That was bad.

But if the experience had warranted the label of worst day since she'd come to Egypt, her current situation trumped that epithet. She found herself in a crowded room that smelled of limestone and dark spices, and judging by her company, the guards had made a terrible mistake.

She rubbed her sleepy eyes and took in the others around her. It wasn't just her tattered, filthy garments that made her stand out like Zeus's lightning bolt; she was the only woman in the group, and based on appearances, these men were important. *Sau* priests if the leopard skins draped over their shoulders was any indication. Powerful magicians. Each was completely shaven of all body hair, as was the custom. Dressed in light linen, they sparkled from their bald heads to their bare toenails. She'd never been that clean in her life.

Suddenly she realized the source of the scent she'd noticed when she arrived. Not dark spices but anointing oils. The priests gave her a disapproving look, and she moved away from them to huddle on the far side of the room.

She did not belong here. Not only was she not a priest, she wasn't even Egyptian. Alena hailed from Crete, Greece, a commoner who had taken to the healing arts. She'd only made the perilous journey to Egypt to study in the library of Alexandria. Herbs and pharmacopoeia were her passion, and she wished to learn what knowledge the books and scrolls there contained. The library had almost burned down once. It was her life's dream to investigate what it had to offer before some other disaster challenged its stacks.

Her father had begged her not to go. He'd become

dependent on her in many ways, the least of which was to fill the hole that had been left when her mother died. But two seasons ago she'd realized she would never leave Crete or realize her potential as a healer if she didn't seek passage to the greatest source of knowledge her generation had ever known.

Thank the gods her talents had proven lucrative. Quickly she had taken to tending the sick and acting as a midwife. News of her competence had traveled far and wide and earned her the sobriquet of Healer of the Nile. And although it was dirty work and she was rarely paid in coin, her calling had provided a suitable dwelling and a full belly.

At least the presence of the priests in this stone room meant she wasn't in any real danger. Why would Cleopatra imprison her own sorcerers? This was either a misunderstanding or some sort of royal request for services. Perhaps the pharaoh was in need of healing. She tried to remain calm and take comfort in the fact that she was in the company of important men, not criminals.

"Well, well, well. If it isn't the Healer of the Nile," a man said from behind her.

Her spine stiffened. She knew that voice. She hated that voice. She closed her eyes and sighed before turning to face him.

"Orpheus, the louse charmer." She shot the man a slanted glance. Like her, Orpheus stood out from the others in the room, although his clothing was also of far better quality than hers. His thick black hair and short beard contradicted the clean-shaven heads of the others, and he was certainly *not* a priest. A smooth-talking charlatan maybe, but not a priest.

By profession, he was a popular barber, one who claimed the rare distinction of successfully ridding heads of vermin without having to shave them. The skill was all but unheard of, and people came from everywhere for his services. Truly, it was a shame a man of such talent and wealth had the personality of a pimple on the ass of a diseased rat.

"Why the hostility, Alena? You're not still mad about what happened between us?" He flashed his most disarming smile.

She silently cursed as her insides reacted with a reflexive rush of lightning. The man was devastatingly handsome with the tawny glow of one blessed by the gods. In other circumstances, she would feel quite honored to have garnered his attention, she'd give him that. Dark-haired and blue-eyed, he had a mouth that seemed locked in a permanent smirk. She'd made the mistake of kissing that mouth, an act akin to drinking sweet poison.

An exasperated sigh tore from her lips. "Did *you* have something to do with this? You did something stupid, didn't you, and then likely threw out *my* name as an alibi!"

"No!" He scoffed.

She spread her hands and gestured toward the

priests, who were doing their best to ignore them properly. "Then why are *we* here?"

"No idea, but we are the only ones in this room not employed by Cleopatra. These men are magicians, sorcerers, priests. They tend to the gods. It seems odd they've summoned us as well."

"My thoughts exactly." Alena hated to agree with Orpheus about anything, but she was hard-pressed to come up with any explanation.

Their conversation was interrupted by the heavy grinding of stone on stone. Alena whirled to find soldiers sliding a heavy slab into the doorway, completely sealing off the exit. With no windows or alternate ways out of the tiny room, Alena instantly felt choked off.

"Stop! What are you doing?" She lurched toward the door, but Orpheus caught her by the arms.

"Those swords aren't for show, Alena. Whatever they have in store for us, you won't avoid it that way."

"But... but... we're trapped in here." Pain flared in her chest, and her breath came in ragged pants.

"Easy." Orpheus rubbed her shoulders. Her wild eyes found his and he guided her through some deep breaths. "Keep your wits about you. We're going to need them."

Slowly her panic abated. Despite being a rake and a scoundrel, Orpheus was an important man in Alexandria. Surely she was safe here among the priests and him. A half dozen torches mounted above their heads bathed them in flickering shadows.

"I can't even make out the door we came through," Alena said.

"Odd that." Orpheus grimaced, showing a mouthful of suspiciously straight white teeth. No other man, Greek or Egyptian, sported such a perfect smile. She wondered for the hundredth time what bargain he'd struck with the gods to maintain his impossibly good looks.

"Can't you charm a louse to squeeze through the walls and get us out of here?" Alena said through her teeth, annoyed by his nearness. She crossed her arms between them and tapped her foot expectantly in his direction.

"If there was a louse among this hairless crew, yes I could."

"I have hair."

He arched a brow. "And we both know that thanks to your herbal concoctions, there isn't a single louse on you either. Although what a tiny insect could do to open a stone door anyway, I have no idea. Unfortunately, there isn't a single living thing in this room that would be any help in getting us out of it."

She shook her head. "As expected, a bastion of self-importance but completely useless in a crunch."

He recoiled from the insult but recovered soon enough. "What about you, Alena? Don't you have anything in that bag that could help us?" He glared at the satchel at her hip.

She didn't go anywhere without her apothecary basket, and she'd felt fortunate when the guards had allowed her to bring it. Inside, she stored a wide variety of herbs and elixirs in small glass jars or wrapped in parchment.

She placed a protective hand over it. "Only if we all come down with fever."

Nonchalantly, he leaned a shoulder against the wall and crossed his legs at the ankle. "As expected. Asserts to raise the dead but completely useless in an emergency."

"I never said I could raise the dead! Oh, you're a child." She turned her back to him, a welcome surge of anger and frustration driving out her previous fears.

"Frankly, I'm surprised the soldiers allowed you to bring your apothecary," he murmured thoughtfully.

She turned back to him. "It was unusual. At the time, I assumed someone in the palace needed healing, but clearly that's not why I'm here." Her eyes narrowed on him.

"Why are *you* here anyway? Didn't you tell Cleopatra's guards that you're an archon of Athens, invited here as an advisor by the pharaoh herself?"

His face fell at her reference to the lie he'd used to try to take advantage of her. "I never said I was an archon. You assumed."

She clenched her teeth. "Only because you had

suggested as much on the boat to Alexandria. The elaborate clothing, the food, the servants. It all seemed to indicate you were an important government official, a leader."

"As I recall, you benefited frequently from my generosity."

She couldn't deny it. He had been generous, and at the time that generosity had meant everything to her.

"The crew of the vessel said you were the eponymous archon of Athens. Who would have told them such if not you? And you did not refute it, although you must have heard the rumors."

"Is it my duty to correct every wagging tongue? Athens has a council of archons, not a single magistrate. You should have known it was a falsehood."

"You knew and you allowed me to believe it. It was under that presumption that I allowed you to woo me within a hair's breadth of your bed, only to discover in the most embarrassing way that it was all a lie."

For weeks he'd pursued her, bringing her gifts, sharing long walks, even doing his best to bump into her at the market. But then he'd invited her to a feast at the home of a prominent Alexandrian. It was there that a group of elderly wives had pulled her aside and told her the truth. He was the louse charmer—their name for the barber—and she was one of many women he'd wooed under false pretenses. He was a cad, a rake, and a scoundrel. The old women had wasted no time sharing their deep regret that her reputation among the elite was already scarred by arriving on his arm.

"I pursued you because I enjoyed your company." He gave her a wicked half smile. "Not only to bed you."

"He flirts with every woman in the city," she said, mimicking the voice of the old women. "He's a scoundrel, a cheater. Allow him between your legs and it will be the last time he gives you any attention whatsoever."

"Untrue. You can't believe such things." He raised an eyebrow.

"Oh?" She planted her fists on her hips. "And the woman I saw coming out of your abode on the last moon?"

He opened his mouth but stopped short. His gaze lifted toward the ceiling. "Not that I don't love debating the history of our meeting and my scandalous behavior once again, but does it appear to you that the smoke is gathering?"

Alena glanced upward to find a thick cloud building above them. "The torches. There's no ventilation." The small, windowless room was growing warmer as well. Already her eyes stung, and the air appeared cloudy between them. "There isn't enough space and too many mouths breathing. Orpheus, if this keeps building..." She gave him an ominous look.

He inhaled deeply and muttered something inaudible under his breath.

One of the priests tested the door. As she

suspected, it was sealed. Alena couldn't even see the outline of the opening in the stone. Another priest pounded on the walls and cried for help. Still another tried to scale the wall to put out one of the torches, but the brace was set too high and caged in iron. Worse, Alena noticed more smoke coming through the stone up above.

"They're doing this on purpose!" she cried, gathering a loose bit of fabric from the neck of her cloak and pressing it around her mouth and nose. Did Cleopatra mean to kill them all?

The smoke thickened by the minute. The walls were too close, the air too tight. True fear pulverized her resolve to stay calm, and the shaking in her knees spread to the rest of her body. Orpheus tugged on her hand, gesturing for her to sit. Considering her knees were about to give out anyway, she dropped to the rough, mercifully cool floor. The air was cleaner there, and she drew in a panicked breath.

"Alena, it's a test," Orpheus said with utmost certainty.

She stared at him with stinging eyes, willing her addled brain to understand what he was talking about. To her surprise, he didn't seem to be struggling to breathe at all. Nor was he panicked as she was.

"What kind of test?" she rasped. "One to see who can hold their breath the longest? I fear we will all fail. Cleopatra may be the reincarnation of Isis, but the rest of us are only human."

"Are you?" Orpheus's eyes crinkled at the corners.

"Aren't *you*?" Alena's gaze connected with his through the smoky air.

One of the priests banged on the wall in earnest now, his pleas for release growing as he struggled for air, while still others slumped or crawled on their bellies, anything for a small measure of comfort. She lowered her chest to the floor. Orpheus followed, although the smoke didn't seem to be bothering him anyway.

"Haven't you noticed that everyone in this room has a reputation for magic?" he asked.

"Not everyone. I do not advertise myself as such." She coughed into her cloak.

"Ah, but it is known, Alena. You are the healer they say can make a tonic to cure any ill. Some call you a hedge witch."

She coughed violently. "Those who wish to be healed should stop making up names for me."

"But they aren't wrong, are they?"

A priest who'd balanced on the shoulders of another to try to extinguish one of the torches fell unconscious to the stone floor. His head cracked near her hand. Blood ran from his fractured skull, scoring a deep crimson river in the stone. Alena shuffled away from it. Her instinct was to dig in her basket and find something to try to heal him, but she could hardly breathe herself. They were all doomed. All but Orpheus, who hadn't coughed once.

"You believe this is a test of our abilities? Someone is trying to prove we have... magic?"

His lips pursed and he gave a curt nod. "It would be a particularly gruesome horror to watch a woman as beautiful as you die. I'd much prefer your company under sweeter circumstances. I enjoyed our time together up until those crones ruined everything with their lies. More than I can say." He grabbed her arm and gave her a hard shake. "Come on, Alena. Think. Tell me you have something in that bag you can use. How hard can it be? All you have to do is survive."

Her throat and eyes burned and her lungs spasmed with their need for air. She cursed. Why wasn't he as affected as she? He still wasn't coughing, and his eyes glowed an arresting shade of lapis in the dingy room. She shook her head and concentrated. He was right. She was a powerful healer. There must be something she could use to protect herself from the smoke if she could calm herself long enough to remember how to use it. Digging in her basket, she drew a length of aeras lily root and wove a braid of Nile grasses around it. Muttering a spell, she formed the resulting mask into a shallow bowl and cupped it over her mouth and nose. Instantly, she could breathe again.

"Aeras root. I hadn't thought of that."

"I developed this spell for a boy in the village who has trouble breathing during the dry season. I wouldn't have thought to use it if you hadn't..." She stopped. She wouldn't give him the satisfaction. "What did you use?"

"Containment spell. I'm inside a sophisticated barrier. Although, to be honest, I didn't think it through. The air is getting thin in here. If this test goes on much longer, I may be joining our friends." He gestured to the priests who were now writhing on the floor, either coughing or limp and unconscious. "I can't renew the spell without any fresh air to seal around myself."

Alena could see it now, how the smoke never seemed to actually touch Orpheus. It curled away from his flesh. Genius, she thought. She'd love to ask him about that particular spell if they ever got out of this room.

"How long have you known about me?" she asked.

"Since the feast. When I kissed you, I knew you were magic. Couldn't you sense it in me?"

She searched his face. The kiss had sent tingles through her body, but it wasn't as though she'd had anything to compare it to. Weren't all kisses like that? She shook her head.

Orpheus shrugged and started to cough. "Hades, it seems my spell is wearing off. And no closer to finding out what Cleopatra wants from us, other than to die."

No one could claim to know the mind of Cleopatra. Far above the commoners of Egypt, her will was a maze of secrets known only to her. Alena had always thought it would be lonely to be a pharaoh; perhaps that was why it wasn't hard to believe the rumors that Cleopatra's obsessive quest for power had made her a killer. Some said she'd murdered her own brother for the throne.

Orpheus pressed his face into his hands, body stretched out on the floor. She had to make a difficult decision. Did she assume this trial must have one winner and allow the smoke to overcome him? Or did she help him and risk inviting the wrath of Cleopatra?

In the end, there was no decision to make. It was bad enough to live with the knowledge that she could do nothing to help the other men who'd collapsed in the room. Refusing aid to Orpheus when he was the reason she'd thought to build the mask in the first place would be a black mark on her soul she could not abide.

Alena took a deep breath and then moved her mask to cover Orpheus's nose and mouth. His body eased beside her, his breathing evening out. He took three long breaths, then moved the mask back to her face. They survived together, sharing the mask, until the smoke was so thick she could no longer see the walls of the room, only his deep-blue eyes.

And then the stone-on-stone rumble filled the room again. Not the door this time. Like a dream, one entire wall of their cell slid away. Cool air wafted around them. The smoke rose up and out in a billow of gray. Light cut through the foggy air. Orpheus had her by the shoulders and was helping her to her feet.

She blinked rapidly. Through the dispelling haze, she could make out a vast hall ahead of them with brightly painted columns. Colorful tapestries draped the walls, and a long red rug led to a dais. She squinted to make out who or what was on that platform at the other end of the room, but her eyes still stung from the smoke, and their watering blurred her vision. Alena leaned into Orpheus, and together they hobbled along the aisle. Fire burned in a series of great gold bowls lighting their way. Alena blinked and blinked again.

Dread filled her heart when she realized who it was on that platform, sitting on her golden throne. Not some soldier or priest or counselor as she'd expected but Cleopatra herself.

Her hair was as black and shiny as the Nile at midnight, and her clothing was solid gold. Everything about her was fashioned to intimidate her subjects, from the robe made to resemble the feathers of Isis to the headdress of horns that framed a large red disk that reflected the light of the flickering torches in a way that seemed supernatural.

Alena swallowed hard. This woman ruled Egypt. She truly might be a goddess for all Alena knew. She definitely held their lives in her hands. It was said she was beautiful, but Alena didn't see beauty, only power. She radiated it like a deadly, burning sun.

Orpheus tugged her shoulders as they arrived at the base of the dais, and she followed his lead, dropping to her knees beside him.

An elderly man who stood beside the pharaoh announced, "All hail Cleopatra, the embodiment of Isis, sister to Horus and Ra, and queen of all Egypt."

Alena lowered her forehead to the floor and prayed to all the gods whose names she could remember that the worst was already behind her.

Continue the story —>

ACKNOWLEDGMENTS

The Angel of Paragon would not exist if not for several readers in my Wicked Readers VIP group who requested—no demanded—Charlie's love story. I hope you all are please with the results. Thank you for being so passionate about this one.

Another big thank you to Anne at Victory Editing. Your edits always bring the best out of my stories.

To author Sara Whitney, I so appreciate you beta reading this one. I can always count on you and am so lucky to have you in my circle.

And finally, Deranged Doctor Designs, thank you for working with me on the cover. Every one you do for me is better than the last.

MEET GENEVIEVE JACK

USA Today bestselling and multi-award winning author Genevieve Jack writes wild, witty, and wicked-hot paranormal romance and romantic fantasy. She believes there's magic in every breath we take and probably something supernatural living in most dark basements. You can summon her with coffee, wine, and books, but she sticks around for dogs and choco-late. Her novels feature badass heroines, fiercely loyal heroes, and fantasy elements that will fill you with wonder. Learn more at GenevieveJack.com.

Do you know Jack? Keep in touch to stay in the know about new releases, sales, and giveaways. https://www.genevievejack.com/newsletter/

facebook.com/AuthorGenevieveJack

instagram.com/authorgenevievejack

bookbub.com/authors/genevieve-jack

tiktok.com/@Genevievejackbooks

twitter.com/genevieve_jack

MORE FROM GENEVIEVE JACK!

His Dark Charms Duet

Lucky Me

Lucky Us

The Treasure of Paragon

The Dragon of New Orleans, Book 1

Windy City Dragon, Book 2,

Manhattan Dragon, Book 3

The Dragon of Sedona, Book 4

The Dragon of Cecil Court, Book 5

Highland Dragon, Book 6

Hidden Dragon, Book 7

The Dragons of Paragon, Book 8

The Last Dragon, Book 9

The Angel of Paragon, Book 10

The Three Sisters Trilogy

The Tanglewood Witches

Tanglewood Magic

Tanglewood Legacy

Knight Games

The Ghost and The Graveyard, Book 1

Kick the Candle, Book 2

Queen of the Hill, Book 3

Mother May I, Book 4

Logan (companion novel)

Fireborn Wolves Trilogy

Vice, Book 1

Virtue, Book 2

Vengeance, Book 3